Tansy glanced up to find his grey eyes on her, with an expression in them she understood. And the feeling in her chest seemed to swell, until she could hardly breathe. This wasn't meant to happen! Surely Nicholas couldn't feel like that about her? She'd never encouraged him. In fact, she'd frequently seen him in the company of one of the staff nurses, and had assumed some sort of relationship there. Now he was looking at her in a way she remembered only too well, like Rod——

How could she cope if he said he loved her? Oh, lord, she'd never envisaged this happening again! And really—she felt a lump in her throat—did she really want to turn him down, reject his friendship, even his love?

Alice Grey attended Queen Mary's High School in Walsall, and really intended to be an artist! She did nursing training instead, followed by midwifery and health visiting while her two sons were small. She has been writing since the age of fourteen, but Medical Romances are a recent change of direction for her, and she wishes she had started them sooner.

Alice Grey lives on the borders of Birmingham and Worcestershire, with her husband and two cats. Her interests are reading, painting, logic problems and amateur dramatics. She also teaches creative writing.

Previous Title

THE BABY DOCTORS

TANSY'S
CHILDREN

BY

ALICE GREY

MILLS & BOON LIMITED
ETON HOUSE   18–24 PARADISE ROAD
RICHMOND   SURREY   TW9 1SR

CHAPTER ONE

THE wind tugged at Tansy's skirt and blew her corn-gold hair around her face, as she hurried towards the entrance of Outpatients. Rain had been threatening for some time, and the first large drops fell on her green suede jacket as she pushed open the doors.

The smells and sounds that assailed her, frightening to many people, were familiar and friendly to Tansy. Hospital was a second home to her. And, after a traumatic week's break, spent in the Lake District, it was like coming home. A surge of adrenalin ran through her body. She could hardly wait to get started.

As she crossed the hall she was aware of the busy activity in the patients' canteen on her left, and could smell the coffee, the cheese and onion crisps, the chocolate bars. It reminded her that she hadn't had time for a proper breakfast, just a glass of orange juice. Not a good example to the patients!

On her right a knot of anxious people gathered at the reception desks, where the calm, unhurried clerks gave out appointments and advice and helpful information. One woman, tapping impatiently on the counter top as the clerk dealt with a deaf old man, caught Tansy's eye as she crossed the floor to the stairs. A smile transformed her disgruntled features.

'Dr Blair——'

Tansy gave her a quick smile, mouthed 'hello', and started up the stairs before the woman, smile frozen, could reach her. She couldn't help feeling that seeing Mrs Lawrence was not an auspicious omen for the day. And she felt a little guilty at her curt behaviour. But she had smiled at her, she had returned her greeting. There would no doubt be ample time to talk to her when she saw Désirée later in the day. Mrs Lawrence would make sure there was. Désirée. Never had a girl been blessed with such an unfortunate name. Désirée—desired. The only one who could ever desire her was her mother, her father having long disappeared from the scene.

Tansy wondered briefly why Mrs Lawrence was here so early. There'd been no sign of Désirée. Probably buying crisps and chocolate bars from the WRVS canteen. More spots, more pounds. Although a few more couldn't make much difference.

Tansy glanced at her watch as she reached the top of the stairs. Nine-fifteen, Tuesday, and a typical, blustery April day. Surely she'd never seen Désirée Lawrence on a Tuesday before? And surely never before the midday appointment? She couldn't remember changing it, couldn't remember any reason for changing it. Hadn't Mrs Lawrence always insisted that poor Désirée couldn't possibly come earlier, she always felt so terrible in the mornings? Her innocent choice of words had made Tansy smile to herself, and then she'd felt uncharitable to the poor girl. Terrible in the mornings. It had just seemed to Tansy that Désirée was extremely unlikely to be in the condition that led to one's feeling terrible in the mornings. A boyfriend? A husband? It seemed impossible right now.

Tansy's throat suddenly contracted painfully. Unaccountably, she felt a sudden empathy with the fat, plain Désirée.

'Just the person I wanted to see!' A hand reached out and grabbed her sleeve as she started along the right arm of the corridor, where a sign read 'CHILD PSY-CHIATRY'. She turned, and her violet eyes met the smoky grey ones of paediatrician Nicholas Vernon.

'Nicholas!'

'You look well. Did you have a nice holiday?' For a moment she felt he suspected. His gaze was intense, and she felt a thudding in her chest.

'It was lovely, thanks. But I——'

'Can I see you later?'

'Well——'

'It's very important—personal. Could we have lunch together? About one?'

Tansy felt she was being swept away. 'If it's that important, of course.' She flashed him a smile, a professional smile. He released his grip.

'Are you seeing one of my referrals today?' he asked.

'Am I? I couldn't say. Haven't seen my list yet.'

'Her name's Debbie Ross. She's eleven, and vomiting. I can't seem to find a damn thing wrong with her—all tests negative. I hope to God I haven't missed something vital.'

He spoke anxiously, and Tansy was aware, as she frequently was, of his dedication to his young patients. He ran his fingers through his thick chestnut hair and grinned at her.

'Here I go again, telling you, when it's all down in black and white. It's just—a feeling I have about it. A feeling about the mother.'

'Perhaps she's the one who needs the therapy,' Tansy suggested lightly. A family therapist was employed by the hospital, a highly skilled woman with a grown-up family of her own. Tansy had found her extremely useful in helping parents to understand their offspring's problems.

'One o'clock, then?' Again, a fleeting look of anxiety crossed his strong features.

'Sure.'

She hurried along the corridor and entered the child psychiatric unit, brightly decorated with Walt Disney characters, furnished with turquoise and cerise chairs and tables, boxes of toys, shelves of books.

'Morning, Dr Blair,' called the pretty receptionist at the window, as she sorted files and answered the phone at the same time. 'Nice holiday?'

'Lovely, thanks.' Tansy paused at the window.

'Did you want something, Doctor?'

'Look at my list, Pam, will you? Have I put Désirée Lawrence down for this morning?'

'Désirée—but she doesn't come Tuesdays, Dr Blair. And never before midday.'

'I know that. Will you look?'

'Sure.' Pam shuffled the papers. 'No, Doctor, she's not down for today. Nor Thursday either. Do you want me to——'

'No, it's all right, Pam, thank you.'

Relieved, Tansy left her jacket in the small staff cloakroom, and, after combing through her chin-length wavy hair, she went across to her consulting-room and sat at her desk.

No Désirée Lawrence today. What she really meant was, no Mrs Lawrence. The woman really was a pain in the neck, and it was becoming increasingly difficult not to show it. So it was a load off her mind. So why was she still feeling tense? As if something momentous was about to happen? Why was adrenalin surging through her body again? It wasn't just because she was eager to get back to work. She wasn't planning anything different today, just meeting Nicholas in the dining-room for lunch—something that happened often.

'Personal', he'd said. And he'd seemed worried. Well, it was unlikely he was needing the attention of a child psychiatrist, he was far too old! Over thirty, she imagined. No, it had to be some other personal problem he had. Though why he imagined she could help him was beyond her.

Her list for the morning, with the files, was waiting on her desk. Her first appointment, for nine-thirty, was Debbie Ross, the child Nicholas had referred. She glanced at her watch. Nine-twenty. Ten minutes to learn what she could about the child before calling them in. Ruefully, she remembered the letter in her shoulder-bag, the letter from America.

Well, Mother, you'll just have to wait, she said to herself. You'll have to wait until I've got ten minutes to spare. She opened the file.

Debbie Ross was eleven, height four feet ten inches, weight five stone two pounds. Bright, in her first year at the local secondary school, she seemed to be coping well, and did not admit to any problems. Mrs Ross, a devoted mother, had been naturally concerned when she found her daughter vomiting in the bathroom. Debbie had admitted she was frequently sick.

Nicholas had elicited a number of facts, among them the statement by the girl that she didn't suffer from nausea, the vomiting came on suddenly after most meals, there was no abdominal pain or tenderness. All the usual tests had been done, and proved negative. In short, there didn't appear to be anything physically wrong.

There was no mention in the notes of Nicholas's intuition about the mother, but then medicine wasn't about intuition, it was about facts. Tansy was the one who had to apply intuition.

There were a few details in the notes about the child's interests—reading, embroidery, knitting, ballet. Well, she certainly seemed to have the build of a ballet dancer, Tansy decided, checking the girl's height and weight. Perhaps a little underweight, but not surprising if she was vomiting a good deal.

Tansy sat back in her chair and pressed the button for the first patient. Within seconds she heard the swing doors and footsteps in the corridor, one pair sharp and incisive, the other barely audible. The door was rapped sharply, and before Tansy could answer it was pushed open and Mrs Ross strode confidently into the room. Behind her, Debbie, a pale child with light brown hair and big blue eyes, hesitated in the doorway.

'Good morning, Dr Blair. I'm Mrs Ross. I must say, you look very young to be a psychiatrist.' She turned and almost pulled Debbie towards the desk. 'This is Debbie. Sit down, Debbie, and don't bite your nails.'

The girl perched on the edge of the chair anxiously, her eyes cast down, her hands restless in her lap. Mrs Ross seated her well-corseted figure in the other chair and leaned forward to make her point.

'Let me just make one thing clear, Doctor. I'm here under duress. Debbie is here under duress. There's nothing wrong with Debbie's mind, she's a bright girl, a very talented girl, with an excellent future ahead of her. She has friends, she likes people, the teachers like her, but she does have something wrong with her stomach. And why the other damn fool doctors couldn't find it, I can't imagine. They should be operating, finding out what's really wrong, instead of insisting we come and see you.'

Tansy noticed the use of the word 'we'.

'I'm sorry you feel like this, Mrs Ross. And I see from the file that the other doctors have made extensive tests on Debbie. And if they feel there's a chance her illness may have a psychological basis, don't you think we ought to check it out?'

'You're implying she's mad?'

'I'm not implying anything, Mrs Ross. And I'm not sure what you mean by "mad". If you mean insane—well, looking at Debbie, she doesn't appear to be deranged. But I can't be sure before I've talked with her.'

'You won't need to talk to her,' said Debbie's mother. 'I can tell you anything you want to know.'

Tansy gritted her teeth. 'How old is Debbie?' she asked pleasantly. The child's gaze was fixed on a calendar on the wall, a picture of a clown violinist serenading a ragged child.

'She's eleven. She was eleven in February.'

'Any brothers and sisters?'

'No. We never intended to have children, but—well, she came along when we least expected it. I was——' Mrs Ross flushed'—at an awkward age. But at least she was a girl. I couldn't have stood it if she'd been a boy. Loud, dirty, cheeky creatures! I can't stand boys. But——' her glance rested fleetingly on the child '—she's been everything a little girl should be. Loved her dolls, pretty clothes, and she adores her ballet lessons. The teacher's thrilled with her progress. Oh, yes, she's a proper little lady. I don't think I could have stood it if she'd been one of those tomboys who like to wear boys' clothes—jeans.'

From where she sat, Tansy could see the restless movements of Debbie's hands, and had plainly noticed the badly bitten nails, the torn cuticles. Mrs Ross obviously didn't feel these defects spoiled her image of her daughter. Tansy was very quickly beginning to understand Nicholas's anxious feeling about the case. There was certainly 'something about the mother'. Tansy couldn't help wondering if Debbie's vomiting was a symbolic 'being sick of her mother'. It was something she had to bear in mind.

'Debbie has a father, I see,' she said, reading the file.

'Of course she does!'

'And what does he think of it all? Is he worried about Debbie's illness?'

Mrs Ross looked surprised. 'I wouldn't really know. He has nothing to do with Debbie. How can a man understand a little girl?'

'Nothing to do with her at all?'

'He spends most of his time at the office. He has to. He has a business—computers. He's always put in long hours to keep us financially secure. I've brought Debbie up. Isn't that what a mother's for? Debbie has wanted for nothing.'

Mrs Ross sat back and folded her arms. Tansy felt she was trying to break through a brick wall. She copied the woman's gesture.

'Did her father enjoy her company when she was small?' she asked.

Mrs Ross frowned. 'Oh, no. Like myself, he didn't plan on having a family. He was quite content to leave Debbie to me. And——' she puffed out her ample chest '—for one who was not prepared for a child, I feel I've done an admirable job. Don't you agree?'

Tansy sought hard for a tactful reply. 'I'm sure Debbie has turned into just the child you wanted,' she said. Mrs Ross missed the hidden implications, and smiled.

'Well, let's get started,' she said abruptly. 'What do you want to know?'

'I'd like to know what Debbie thinks about it all.'

'Debbie? But I told you——'

'Mrs Ross, it's my practice to see a family together at the beginning. And I believe your appointment letter did ask your husband to come.' Mrs Ross opened her mouth, but Tansy went on, unheeding.

'And then I have to talk to the child. Alone.'

For an instant Debbie's eyes lifted and met hers, and she was shocked at the expression in them.

'You want to see Debbie alone?'

'It's the usual practice. She is the patient, and as she's perfectly capable of talking, I feel I ought to hear her opinions.'

'She's only eleven, Dr Blair. She can't know her own mind.'

'She's an intelligent girl', said Tansy quietly. 'Many of my patients are much younger than Debbie, but they manage to give me a very clear picture of what's bothering them. So, if you don't mind, Mrs Ross, perhaps you'd wait in the waiting-room? We may be a little while, so perhaps you'd care to get a cup of tea from the canteen?'

The wind seemed to have been taken out of Mrs Ross's sails. She shifted in her chair, glancing at Debbie, who steadfastly refused to look at her.

'Will she be all right?'

'Of course she'll be all right,' said Tansy with some asperity. 'I'm not going to eat her!'

A soft giggle escaped Debbie. Mrs Ross glared at her, stood up and straightened her skirt.

'I think I'll go and read a magazine,' she said loftily, as though the decision to leave had been hers. Tansy smiled, and the woman, with a last look at the back of her daughter's head, left the room.

Tansy looked up from her notes, at Debbie's pale little face, framed in the straight mousy hair.

'How do you feel about coming to see me, Debbie?' she asked.

The girl shrugged. 'I don't mind.' Her fingers twisted in her lap. 'But I thought you'd be a man!'

Tansy laughed. 'Would you rather see a man?'

'I don't mind.'

'I see from the other doctor's notes—Dr Vernon's notes——' and her heart unaccountably gave a little skip '—that you have a good many hobbies. Which is your favourite?'

'None of them, really.' Debbie's voice was quiet, unemotional.

'You like them all?'

'I don't really like any of them,' the child burst out. There was defiance in the lift of her chin.

'Then why do you do them?'

'Because my mother says I should.'

Tansy digested this. 'So you don't enjoy reading? That surprises me.'

'Oh, reading. Yes, I like reading—that's the only one. But she always chooses my books for me: *Little Women*, *What Katy Did at School*.'

'I always thought they were good books?'

'Good! Everyone's so good in them. I hate them! Little girls who like helping Mother in the house, and doing as they're told, and not allowed to climb trees or swim in rivers, and they lie on couches and cry all the time. Wishy-washy!'

'I see. Don't you ever cry, Debbie?'

'Not when she's around.'

Tansy's pulses quickened. 'Does she upset you?'

'Often. I don't think she was ever a little girl,' added Debbie.

'Yet she says you've always been the perfect daughter.'

'She says that to everybody. But I'm not. I don't always do as she wants. I say things that aren't ladylike. That bit about tomboys in jeans—she knows I want some jeans.'

'You'd like to be a tomboy?'

The girls eyes flashed as she looked at Tansy, and her cheeks had grown pink.

'She won't let me be! She makes me wear awful pink

frocks with lace and bows. I prefer school uniform to the clothes she picks for me.'

Tansy glanced at the smart navy jumper and skirt, and tried to imagine her dressed in frills and flounces. She was really far too plain.

'Have you told her how you feel?' she asked.

'She won't listen.'

Tansy took a deep breath. 'Do you ever say to yourself, "My mother makes me sick!"?' There was a silence. The child stared at the desk.

'What does it say there?' she asked in a small voice. 'I kept telling them, I don't ever feel sick, 'cause the vomiting always comes on suddenly.'

Her face seem to close in on itself. Tansy decided to change her tactics.

'Did you have breakfast this morning, Debbie?'

'I had some porridge. I hate porridge.'

'And have you been sick today?'

Debbie stopped fidgeting. 'We had to come here. Mummy doesn't drive, so we had to get the train, and we didn't want to be late——' She tailed off, and her gaze swivelled to the corner of the room. Tansy stood up.

'I won't be a moment,' she said quietly. 'There's something I've just realised I've forgotten. I'll just run along to the office.'

She slipped out of the room, but didn't go far. Carefully, she tiptoed back to the slightly open door and peeped through the crack. She knew it was unethical to spy on a patient, but she had to see if her suspicions were true.

Debbie was standing at the small washbasin in the corner of the room. As Tansy watched, she pushed her fingers into her throat and was instantly sick. Tansy retreated back along the corridor and called back to an invisible person.

'Thank you, Pamela. I'm getting so absent minded!' She made as much noise as she could as she went back into her office. Debbie was running the water, and dabbing at her mouth with a tissue.

'Anything wrong?' asked Tansy kindly.

'I've just been sick,' said Debbie, quite cheerfully, and returned to her chair. Tansy sat back and looked at her, and a surge of pity ran through her.

'Debbie,' she said slowly 'I think we'd better have a long talk, you and I.'

It was quarter past ten when Debbie left with her mother, and Tansy felt quite exhausted. Mrs Ross had demanded she be told what had passed between Tansy and her daughter, and it had taken all of the doctor's powers of diplomacy to refuse her request.

'I'm sure I can help Debbie,' she told her. 'And with everyone's help it shouldn't take too long.'

She had not revealed to the child what she had seen. She wanted the girl to tell her herself. Likewise, she had not told Mrs Ross. Not yet, at least.

'I'm sure that's not necessary,' said Mrs Ross. 'If she has problems, she'll soon tell me, won't you Debbie?'

Debbie cast an agonised glance at Tansy.

'Mrs Ross, I feel it would be better all round if you don't question Debbie,' said Tansy. 'I'm sure she'll tell you in her own time. I'd like her to come next Tuesday at ten. Is that all right?'

'She has to come every week?'

'For the moment. And I'd like to see Mr Ross too. Will you tell him?' Tansy glanced at her watch. 'Now, I have another patient——' She ushered them into the corridor.

'Oh, if we must. I have nothing planned for Tuesday.' Huffily, Mrs Ross led Debbie along the corridor. Sighing, Tansy went back to her room. If only children didn't have to have parents! She caught her breath. Some children didn't. She tightened her lips and pressed the buzzer for the next patient.

But it was Pamela who came into the room, bearing a mug of coffee.

'Mrs Downes has cancelled, Dr Blair,' she said, placing it on the desk. 'She just rang up. Paula's got chickenpox.'

'You'd better send her another appointment for two weeks. Is the ten-thirty appointment here yet?'

'Don't think so.'

'Well, I need a bit of a breather. Send him in when he arrives.'

'Will do, Doctor.'

Pam closed the door behind her, and Tansy sat back in her chair and stretched her legs. Her violet eyes looked troubled. She sipped her coffee, but it was too hot. Then she remembered the letter in her bag, tucked under her desk. She pulled it out and tore open the envelope.

'Charlotte, North Carolina, Thursday,' was written in green ink at the top, in a right-sloping hand. She read on with a smile.

Darling Tansy,

By the time you get this letter you'll have come back from your holiday. The Lake District, was it? I always loved the Lake District. I went frequently with your father to Lake Windermere. Of course, there are many pretty places here, but nothing quite like the Lake District. Did you go with Helen?

No, Mother, I went alone. I always go alone at this time of year, and you know why.

There was a very nice small hotel at Windermere, run by a Mrs Greaves, a lovely woman. Nothing too much trouble. She used to go into raptures over my paintings. Of course, that was the real reason we went there—to paint. When are you going to come and see us again? It seems ages since the last time.

We have new neighbours, a young family that moved in last week. Well, quite young. Their names are Richard and Babs. They have the sweetest little girl, she's six, called Francine, and I have to admit, I couldn't help thinking of—well, I won't go into details. I still think you did the wrong thing, but it's your life, after all. And as long as you're happy that's all that matters.

Tansy put down the letter, biting her lip. Another little dig. A gentle tap at the door alerted her to the present. She shoved the letter away, finished her coffee, and called, 'Come in.'

She smiled encouragingly at the teenage boy who sidled diffidently into the room.

'Hello, Gary. Any new stamps?'

The dining-room was full when Tansy arrived, and she couldn't see Nicholas anywhere. She took a tray and joined the queue, trying to focus her mind on the menu, trying to ignore the fluttering in her chest. She chose the cod Mornay because they did a nice cheese sauce here, but refused to look at the mouthwatering but fattening puddings, and took a grapefruit juice instead.

She was fortunate in getting a table for two, tucked away in a corner. Nicholas had said his problem was personal, hadn't he? Problem? Had he said it was a problem? She started her meal, enjoying the tang of the grapefruit on her tongue. And then she saw him, threading his way between the tables, looking for her. She gave a self-conscious wave, and was disturbed by the flush that rose in her cheeks.

'Hi.' As he sat opposite, his gaze rested on her, and her pulses started hammering again. She was furious with herself. This was so—so adolescent! She hadn't felt like this for years, and had no intention of it happening again. So she smiled brightly at him and pretended to be concentrating on her cod Mornay.

'I saw Debbie Ross,' she said lightly. Her gaze rested on his firm hands as he skilfully manoeuvred spaghetti on his fork. She refused to look at his face.

'What did you think?' he asked.

'I think she needs help. You were right about the

mother. I shall very tactfully suggest she talks to the family therapist. But not yet. She's very defensive at the moment.'

'And Debbie's vomiting?'

'I thought it was symbolic at first. But I believe she's a pre-pubertal anorexic.'

Nicholas nodded. Inadvertently, Tansy glanced up, waiting for his reply, only to find his grey eyes on her, with an expression in them she understood. And the feeling in her chest seemed to swell, until she could hardly breathe. This wasn't meant to happen! Surely he couldn't feel like that about her? She'd never encouraged him. In fact, she'd frequently seen him in the company of one of the staff nurses, and had assumed some sort of relationship there. Now he was looking at her in a way she remembered only too well, like Rod——

She put down her fork and wiped her mouth. It was something to do. Her voice was casual as she said, 'What was this—personal problem you wanted to talk about, Nicholas?'

How would she cope if he said he loved her? Oh, lord, she'd never envisaged this happening again! And really—she felt a lump in her throat—did she really want to turn him down, reject his friendship, even his love?

Her eyes dark with anxiety, she looked sympathetically into his face. He seemed troubled.

'Perhaps problem wasn't the right word,' he said, looking away. Then he seemed to make up his mind. He leaned forward. 'Tansy, would you care to come to my home tomorrow evening? For dinner?'

CHAPTER TWO

THERE seemed to be a hammering inside Tansy's head. For a moment she couldn't speak. She folded her paper napkin carefully, and gave a light laugh.

'Dinner, Nicholas? That sounds very nice.'

'Then you'll come?'

'I'll just have to check my diary,' she said jokingly, but a glance at his serious expression made her reach out and touch the back of his hand. 'I was only joking. Of course I'll come. I'd love to.'

'For a moment there I thought——'

'You thought my social life was so full I couldn't fit you in?' Oh, if only he knew the truth! Tansy didn't even need a social diary. She had nothing to put in it. Just the odd date she had to remember, important dates, like April the seventh. A special day. For a brief moment her lips quivered, but Nicholas didn't seem to notice. He had that strangely intense look in his eyes again, and she found herself drawing back, immediately doubting the wisdom of accepting his invitation. Too late now.

'I didn't imagine you as a cook, somehow,' she said, trying to ignore her own response to his expression.

'Oh, I dabble a bit,' he said easily, his gaze still on her. 'Actually, I do have someone who does all that for me.'

'Oh.' A housekeeper, I expect, thought Tansy, and imagined an elderly, motherly woman who clucked over him and made sure he didn't wear damp underwear. And the thought of his underwear made a sudden flush rise up her neck.

'And where is your house?' she asked quickly, trying to focus her mind on the streets of Swindon instead of boxer shorts.

'Ascot Avenue. But you needn't worry about that, I'll come and pick you up.'

'So you know where I live?'

He flushed, and pushed a bit of spaghetti around his plate. 'I—I happened to see you unlocking your front door the other day as I was driving home. One of those Edwardian villas in Vine Road. A blue front door—I couldn't see the number.'

'It isn't all mine,' Tansy admitted, conscious of the difference between her small flat and the houses in Ascot Avenue.

'I didn't imagine it was,' smiled Nicholas. 'No one in their right mind would buy one of those monstrosities to live in themselves.'

'It isn't—well, perhaps you're right. They are ugly. But inside isn't so bad. My flat is very nice.' She wasn't going to let him get away with it wholesale.

'What time shall I pick you up?' he asked.

'You don't really have to, you know. I have a car.'

'I wouldn't dream of it. I made the invitation, so I shall fetch you and take you home. Is six-thirty too early?'

'Not really——' Wouldn't give her much time for a shower and making herself presentable. And what should she wear?

'I have my reasons for suggesting your coming early,' Nicholas said hurriedly. 'It isn't too early for you?'

'No, it's fine.'

Tomorrow would be Wednesday. No afternoon clinic, just the usual ward meeting which was often finished by four o'clock. Perhaps one or two patients to see afterwards. Yes, she could be finished by four-thirty.

'I'm looking forward to it,' she added.

'You don't have any special dislikes, do you?' he asked anxiously. 'You're not a vegetarian, or anything like that, are you? I shall have to tell Beth, you see——'

'Oh, no, I eat pretty well anything,' Tansy reassured him. Beth, was it? Yes, she sounded rather like a mother hen. She could just see her now, in print pinafore over a buxom figure, rosy cheeks flushed from cooking, wisps of greying hair escaping from a bun at the nape of her neck. Yes, Beth sounded nice. Tansy warmed towards her.

She pushed away her plate and half rose. Then she remembered something, and sat again.

'Did you ring me on Sunday, Nicholas?' she asked.

'Ring you? Where?'

'At my flat, of course.'

'But I don't know your address,' he reminded her.

'Of course not.' She had given very few people her number. Had it perhaps been passed on by one of them?

'Weren't you away on Sunday?' Nicholas queried.

'Yes. I came home yesterday. My friend Helen, who's got the next-door flat, said my phone rang for ages on Sunday evening.'

'You thought it might have been me? I don't have your number.'

'No. I can't imagine why I thought it might be you. It can't have been important, or they'd have rung back.'

Nicholas stood up. 'I'll get some coffee.'

And Tansy suddenly realised what an utter fool she'd made of herself. How could it have been Nicholas? Why should it have been Nicholas? And now he would think all the wrong things about her, assume she had expected it to be him. Which was true, of course. Why hadn't she kept her big mouth shut?

He brought the coffee, and Tansy tried to drink hers quickly, even though it was hot. The atmosphere seemed strained now. She knew she had spoiled things; she always did. Must be some sort of defence mechanism, a sort of mental shutter she put up to prevent men getting closer. And she knew why. She was afraid of another relationship. Afraid of how it might end.

Nicholas was talking now about the house and the new bathroom being planned, and Tansy attempted to show an interest.

'I'm not sure if I like these dark colours for bathrooms,' he said. 'Midnight blue—maroon. What do you think, Tansy?'

She crinkled her nose. She did rather like dark blue.

'Peach is nice,' she said tactfully. 'And the colour they call champagne. The names they call them!' She laughed lightly and put down her cup.

'You must tell me what you think,' he said, smiling. 'Beth doesn't agree with me.' Tansy wondered at that remark. Did he need his housekeeper's approval? She stood up.

'I really have to go now,' she said.

'Clinic?'

'We're awfully busy just lately. Lots of new patients.'

'I'm sure you can cope,' Nicholas said warmly, and his gaze met hers again. There was a fluttering in her chest which she couldn't control.

'Flattery,' she said brightly, and turned away.

'See you tomorrow.' She gave him a quick wave and left the room, aware of his gaze on her retreating back. This had to be stopped, she told herself as she went back to her consulting-room. She had all the symptoms of an adolescent crush, and she was twenty-seven! She should never have agreed to his invitation. Yet she couldn't deny that a part of her wanted to go, wanted to be part of his private life.

She was too early for the afternoon session. But it meant she could finish reading her mother's letter. She sat down and pulled it from her bag.

Almost the first words she saw were about the new neighbours. Although 'neighbours' could mean anything up to half a mile away, Tansy mused. She remembered from her last visit, the previous June, that the nearest house was at least a hundred yards down the road, since they all had extensive grounds, swimming pools, the lot.

'They have the sweetest little girl, she's six,' she read again, and quickly turned the page. Francine—almost as fussy a name as Désirée. Strange feelings suddenly overwhelmed her, and she put her head in her hands. Would she never forget? For a moment Rod's face swam into her mind; she could see the way the wind tugged at his black curls, his infectious grin. He could always make her laugh. She'd had nothing to laugh about since.

She brushed away a tear and crumpled the letter in her fist. It was no use dwelling on what might have been, no use filling herself with guilt.

She opened the top file on her desk. Suzanne Barker, aged five, hyperactive. And that was an understatement! The child was almost uncontrollable. Four hours' sleep and she was full of energy, ready to tear the house apart. Tansy really pitied poor Mrs Barker, who already had her hands full with two younger children, and a chauvinistic husband who refused to take a share in what he called 'women's work'.

Tansy flipped through her notes. She had seen Suzanne three times, on successive Tuesdays, and was seriously considering a food allergy as the cause of the child's intractable energy. She had suggested it last week, and exhausted Mrs Barker was only too eager to try anything.

Co-operation was half the battle, thought Tansy. And she was reminded of Debbie Ross. She glanced at her watch. Five minutes to two. The crumpled letter caught her eye. Reluctantly, she spread it out again, and ignored the part she'd read. The rest of the letter was mostly about Ted, her mother's second husband, a man Tansy had never felt entirely at home with. Perhaps, she theorised, when she tried to analyse her feelings, perhaps she laid the blame at his door, for what she had done six years ago—and had regretted ever since. If he hadn't persuaded her mother to emigrate to North Carolina, then things might have been very, very different. . .

Her mother's words were repeated at the end of the letter. 'We both wish you could come and work out here, but as long as you're happy that's all that matters.'

Tansy swallowed hard and pushed the letter into her bag. She pressed the buzzer for the first patient, and fixed a smile on her face. It must have looked genuine, because Mrs Barker responded as soon as she opened the door.

'Hello, Doctor!'

Suzanne galloped into the room and immediately made for the sand tray. Mrs Barker's eyes followed her anxiously, but when Tansy didn't admonish the child for scattering the sand, she turned back, enquiring eyes on the file.

'She's ever so active today, Doctor,' she said, trying to appear cheerful, but her fingers nervously playing with the strap of her shopping bag betrayed her feelings.

'More than usual?'

'I think so. She had Strawberry Pops for her breakfast. She begged and begged me yesterday to get some. I expect it's because it's got those red sugar shapes in it. She saw it on telly, you see, and there was a little girl in it that looked just like her——' She trailed off as Suzanne came running to her with a broken plastic truck in her hands.

'The wheel's come off!' she cried, pummelling her mother's chest.

'I'm awfully sorry, Doctor,' said Mrs Barker apologetically.

'Not to worry,' said Tansy cheerfully. 'Let me see, Suzanne. I'm sure I can put it back.'

But the child had lost interest, and was tipping the bucket of Lego on the floor.

'Red sugar shapes, you said,' Tansy repeated.

'Yes, look like strawberries—very sweet. I tried one.'

'All the children had it for breakfast?'

'Oh, yes, I try to be fair.'

'And the boys aren't hyperactive?'

'Just the opposite. Very placid, they are. I've left them in the hospital crêche. It's a godsend. Pity I can't do the same with Suzanne. She went to nursery school a few times, but they wouldn't keep her. And she's just as bad at her proper school. It was the teacher who insisted I got someone to see her. She was disrupting the class.'

Tansy nodded. It was a familiar story. She smiled sympathetically at Mrs Barker.

'Do you remember what we talked about last week?' she asked.

'That's what I was just saying, Doctor! I think you must be right, about those additives and such. I mean, the colour of those strawberry things—you said some colours had bad effects on some children, and she's certainly been worse this morning——'

She would have gone on and on, in her relief that someone was offering a way out of her predicament, but Tansy interrupted.

'So did you do what I suggested?' she asked.

'You mean, writing down all the things she ate for the last week? Yes, I've got it here. It wasn't easy, trying to remember how she behaved as well, and writing it down, and Alan isn't much help—he seems to think her behaviour is all my fault, and I suppose it is really, since I buy her food——' Mrs Barker realised how she was going on, and rummaged through her vinyl handbag, finally producing a crumpled envelope that had once contained a greetings card. She pulled a sheet of lined paper from it and handed it to Tansy.

'I haven't had a chance to put down this morning's food, but I've told you, haven't I, so you won't forget, will you?'

'No, Mrs Barker, I shan't forget,' said Tansy, unfolding the paper. 'And I really have to admire you for managing to do all this when you really have your hands full.'

Mrs Barker looked gratified, and turned her attention to Suzanne, who had lost interest in the building bricks and was undressing a doll.

Tansy grimaced, and concentrated on deciphering the pencilled handwriting.

Twenty minutes later both Tansy and Mrs Barker had had quite enough of little Suzanne! Tansy was visualising the hospital management committee presenting her with a huge bill for repairs, and poor Mrs Barker did nothing but apologise, unable to control her daughter. Yet

Suzanne could be such a sweet child, thought Tansy,
when she stopped long enough to look at you with those
melting brown eyes.

She rose, handing the list to Mrs Barker. 'These are
the substances that are thought to cause hyperactivity. If
you check all the food you buy for her when you go
shopping, and avoid the ones with those numbers, we
may see some improvement.'

'Oh, I do hope so, Doctor! Suzanne, leave that little
clock alone, you've already pulled a hand off it.'

The child abruptly dropped the toy among the other
rejects, and started to swing the curtains back and forth.

'Same time next week, Mrs Barker,' said Tansy,
returning her green appointment card. 'Time to go,
Suzanne!'

The child ran to the door, dropping a dog-eared book
as she went, and wrenched it open. Before Mrs Barker
could say goodbye, Suzanne was hurtling along the
corridor towards the waiting-room, shouting and squeal-
ing. Mrs Barker's voice floated back to Tansy.

'Thank you, Doctor!'

Tansy gave a sigh of relief and relaxed in her chair.
Ten minutes before the next patient, and it would take
all of that time to clear up the mess Suzanne had made.
Sighing, she got down on her hands and knees and
collected up the Lego. And she found herself comparing
fertile Mrs Barker with the mother of her next patient,
Robert Anderson.

Mrs Anderson was in her late thirties, and after ten
years of childlessness had finally adopted a little boy,
Robert. She idolised the charming, attractive, blond-
haired child, and was finding it extremely difficult to
come to terms with the fact that he was probably
psychopathic, and it was more than likely there was no
chance of a cure.

It was all a gamble, thought Tansy. Whether you had
your own children or someone else's, no one could
possibly know how they were going to turn out. Just a
gamble. Who could know what was in the chromosomes?

As she swept up the last bit of sand and returned it to the tray, a feeling of utter weariness descended on her. What on earth was wrong with her today? She should have sorted out this problem last week, on her annual retreat. She couldn't possibly allow it to affect her working life. It must have been her mother's letter that had started it. She'd felt fine first thing this morning, hadn't she?

She sat at her desk and opened Robert Anderson's file.

There was a good film on television that evening, one she'd always meant to see at the cinema but had somehow missed, so, after checking the time of the programme, Tansy pulled off her crumpled clothes and soaked in a hot, perfumed bath. Her mind kept returning to Nicholas's expression in the dining-room. Could she possibly have misinterpreted it? She hoped, for her sake, she had. She wasn't prepared for that sort of relationship, wasn't sure she'd ever be ready again.

But even as she recalled the intensity in his keen grey eyes and his amused smile, a slow flush crept up her neck and face. And she was glad there was no one to see it!

This is ridiculous! she told herself, as she wrapped a thick white towel around her slim body. This feels like an adolescent crush! And she remembered a time when she was fourteen, obsessed with the boy next door, a leather-clad youth who rode a motorbike, and probably wasn't even aware she existed. She had felt quite devastated when a dark-haired girl in vivid lipstick and high leather boots had clung protectively to him as she rode pillion.

Yes, an adolescent crush, that was all it was. And, given time, she'd get over it. She pulled on her rose-pink dressing-gown and went to make some coffee.

Every Wednesday afternoon a meeting was held on the ward. The Chief, Dr Daniel Rice, was already there when Tansy arrived. He gave her a quick smile and returned to his notes. He was an attractive man in his early forties, tall and broad-shouldered, with touches of silver at his temples, and icy blue eyes. He wasn't liked by the people who couldn't take his blunt manner, and the cold flashes of anger he sometimes showed. But even they had to admit he was a genius with the children, and had achieved success when failure had seemed more than likely. With the children he was a different man, and they loved him, called him Uncle Dan, and even, sometimes, Desperate Dan, after the cartoon character.

He was unattached, although Tansy had heard a rumour that he had been married, a long time ago. But then the hospital was full of rumours, and a good proportion of them had no basis in fact. Still, it could explain his curt behaviour, and his distant manner towards women. Like herself, he kept others at bay. Could he have been betrayed, rejected, perhaps jilted? Was that why he had devoted his life to children, to replace the family he had resigned himself never to have?

Don't be silly, Tansy, she told herself, aware that she was daydreaming. You're just an incurable romantic. Yes, and look where it got you.

'A penny for them,' said a voice at her side. The family therapist, Hattie Strong, plumped down in an easy chair beside her. She eyed with speculation Tansy's distant expression.

'Oh—hello, Hattie. I was just dreaming, that's all.'

'Nice holiday?' Hattie was in her mid-forties, a square-featured, pleasant woman, with twinkling blue eyes and a ready smile. Today she was wearing a blue Paisley dress with a kingfisher brooch pinned to her throat.

'Lovely, thanks,' Tansy told her.

Hattie nodded, looked at her notes before her, and flicked to a clean page of her notebook. She had trained as a nurse, then a midwife, and finally a health visitor, in between getting married and having a daughter, and it was only when a child in her sister's family developed disturbing behaviour that she had realised where her true vocation lay. So she had taken further training to become a family therapist, and with all her past skills she was an invaluable member of the team.

Across the room sat Sister Ellen Chalmers. The decision to hospitalise children with psychological problems was not lightly taken, and most of them who were warded stayed for only short periods. If this wasn't long enough they could be sent to residential units, sometimes for a year or more.

Ellen Chalmers was angular and tall, with fading fair hair tied loosely at the nape of her neck. Like Dr Rice, she could be curt and painfully honest, but everyone who knew her well also knew what a warm heart she had. With a difficult marriage behind her, her life was now the children in her care. She glanced at Tansy and Hattie and smiled. Then she shivered dramatically.

'Have they turned off the central heating?' she asked, but it was a rhetorical question and no one answered.

Dr Rice glanced around him as the social worker and occupational therapist quickly took their seats, smiling apologetically for their last-minute arrival. Dr Rice shuffled his papers.

'Right, perhaps you'd like to begin, Sister.'

Ellen Chalmers cleared her throat. 'Melanie Davies,' she began. 'I'm pleased to say she's calmed down a lot, she's not so aggressive to the others, and she will—occasionally—do things we suggest. So I feel we're getting somewhere. She's still rather abusive to her mother when she visits, and she still tears at her clothes. But I do feel she's improving.'

Hattie Strong broke in. 'Mrs Davies suggested to me that perhaps Melanie might be better if she didn't visit for a while. Does anyone else think this a good idea?'

'Well, certainly, if the mother's attitude is still bad——'

Tansy sat, her hand poised over her notebook, listening as the discussion raged, and occasionally adding suggestions. First Melanie Davies, then Peter Wilson, Shirleen Cox, Jenna Ford—— She jumped, as a pen fell and rolled across the table. With a shock, she realised over an hour had gone by. A number of good suggestions had been made, a number of treatments initiated; two children had been considered well enough to try day patient care.

The room had grown quite warm—it seemed the central heating had not been turned off—and Tansy had begun to feel quite drowsy. Then they'd turned to the new outpatients they'd seen, and, relieved, she spoke about Debbie Ross.

'You'll want me to talk to the parents?' asked Hattie.

'In a week or two,' said Tansy tentatively. 'Mrs Ross has found it difficult enough to come and see me. I shall have to tread very warily. She's finding it hard to come to terms with the fact that her daughter has a psychological problem at all. She'd immediately think we were blaming her if I asked someone else to talk to her. But, given time, I think she'll come round to the idea.'

'And Mr Ross?' asked Hattie.

'Well, that poor man hardly seems part of the family. She seems to find it amazing that I actually want to talk to him as well. I'm hoping he'll come along next week.'

'Let me know,' said Hattie automatically, and pushed her papers together.

The meeting over, they began to organise their notes, talking quietly amongst themselves. Tansy, musing over the Ross family, and Debbie in particular, was suddenly aware that almost everyone else had gone. Everyone except Daniel Rice, who was still seated, reading a report.

Tansy closed her folder, picked up her bag, and moved towards the door. As she passed his chair, about to murmur a word of farewell, Dr Rice looked up.

'Tansy.' She paused, conscious of the scrutiny of his icy blue eyes.

'Did you have a nice holiday?' he asked softly.

'Very nice, thank you.' She turned to go.

'When did you come back?'

'Yesterday. If you remember, I told you——'

He nodded impatiently. 'Yes, yes, I remember now.

It had slipped my mind. You went to the Lake District, I believe.'

'That's right.' She hadn't told him. Who had?

'I expect you're tied up all this week, aren't you?'

'Well, not really——' Only tonight, she thought. He did mean her evenings, didn't he? Surely he knew her days were fully occupied?

He closed the file and stood up. He was tall and broad-shouldered, and his pale blue shirt exactly matched the colour of his eyes.

'I have two theatre tickets,' he said, in his unemotional voice, 'given to me by a grateful parent. Unfortunately, I've been let down at the last moment. I did wonder if you might be interested? The offer includes dinner, of course.'

Tansy tried to read the expression in those pale eyes, but it was impossible.

'It's very kind of you to think of me. When is it——?'

'Tonight.'

Tansy felt a rush of relief that she wouldn't have to lie to him. 'Oh—tonight. I'm awfully sorry——'

'You have a prior engagement. It's quite all right. Very short notice, I'm afraid. I quite understand. An attractive young lady like yourself must have a very busy social life.'

Tansy began to explain, but he cut her short.

'About that autistic boy you saw before you went away, the three-year-old, Richard. Had you decided what would be best——?'

His voice had become curt and professional once again. Tansy felt relieved that he hadn't pursued the subject, but as she glanced at his expression, she found herself feeling sorry for him, and she caught her breath.

Sorry for Daniel Rice? He wasn't the sort of person one did feel sorry for. He was so self-contained, so confident of his own skills. Why did she suddenly feel he was as vulnerable as herself?

Oh, no, no, no, this would never do. Infatuation for Nicholas Vernon. Sympathy—or pity—for Daniel Rice. She would certainly have to watch herself.

And she was suddenly aware that either of those sentiments could easily turn to love. Or be confused with the real thing.

Putting on an air of smiling confidence, she went down to tea.

CHAPTER THREE

THE rain had stopped by the time Tansy left the hospital, although there was a fresh wind which was a portent of more to come. As she drove along the damp streets in her maroon Volvo, she was only too aware of the quickening of her pulse and the dampness of her palms on the steering-wheel. She kept telling herself she was merely having a meal with a colleague. And perhaps Nicholas had invited her just because he felt sorry for her. She was quite new—this was only her tenth week at Greenstead General. Could it be that she didn't appear to have made many friends yet?

That must be it, she insisted, trying to convince herself. That look she had seen in his eyes, it hadn't been anything like she had imagined. Just because Rod had often looked like that. . .

She manoeuvred the car around the side of the house and into a small parking area that had been made at the rear. There wasn't a garage, and she constantly worried that it might get stolen. She tried not to look at the flaking brown paintwork on the rear door and windows, and the crumbling concrete underfoot. She had been very glad to get the flat when she had first come here. The rent was very reasonable.

She walked round to the front and up the steps to the front door. More flaking brown paint, and the yellowing net curtains of Mrs Makepeace on the ground floor. Yes, it was time she found somewhere else. Nicholas had been right: the house was a monstrosity. And she could really afford something better, nearer to the hospital. Yet, in the short time she had been here, she had made lots of improvements to her own small flat. It was quite cosy now, a nice place to retreat to when she wanted to relax.

Retreat—that word again. Tansy ran up the stairs and unlocked her door.

When she finally emerged from the bathroom, her damp golden hair clinging in tendrils to her neck, her cheeks pink, the clock was showing five forty-five. Excitement began to rise in her, and she could feel her heart pounding. She tried to stop it, but it was no use. Why had she allowed herself to feel like this about him? He wasn't anything special, after all, quite ordinary-looking, with thick chestnut hair, warm grey eyes—although he did have nice long eyelashes, and beautifully shaped eyebrows, she recalled.

Stop it, stop it! she told herself. You're letting your feelings run away with yourself. You'll have to be careful you don't let him see how you feel. So silly to wear your heart on your sleeve. Look what happened last time. . .

She plugged in her hair-dryer, and hummed to herself as she brushed her hair into a soft waving style. She was determined to keep this relationship—if it ever became one—on a purely friendly basis. She could see now where she had gone wrong last time. Her mother had been right—throwing herself at him, she'd called it. But Tansy, at nineteen, had been typically contrary and rebellious, and hadn't listened. Well, she'd learned her lesson the hard way.

'The hardest way of all,' she whispered, as she applied make-up in front of her dressing-table mirror. 'Now, whatever you do, don't cry, or that mascara will run!' She blinked the tears away furiously.

No, she was going to be resolute and determined. Nothing was going to spoil her life again. She picked up her lipstick.

She had decided to wear a plum velvet dress with a demure round neck and white lace collar, and only the minimum of make-up in pink and pale violet. A touch of perfume, her favourite Opium, and she was ready.

It was almost time. She slipped her new silver-grey coat around her shoulders, catching sight of her image in the hall mirror, and smiled at herself. She felt quite pleased with what she saw.

The doorbell rang, and her heart fluttered. Trying to appear calm and in control, she locked her flat and went down the stairs.

Nicholas was wearing a brown suede jacket over a lemon shirt and beige cords. He seemed taller than usual to Tansy, taller and broader, and she found herself noticing a small dimple in his chin. She hadn't been aware of it before. For a moment they looked at each other, and that same intent message seemed to be in his eyes. She felt herself drawing back.

'Ready?' he asked.

'You said half-past six, and as a doctor I'm used to being punctual.'

'I was hoping we could forget about being doctors,' he said lightly, his hand on her shoulder. 'For an hour or so, at least.'

'Of course,' said Tansy, trying to keep the quiver out of her voice.

She followed him to his car, a gold-coloured Mercedes, and he opened the door for her. She settled herself in the dark brown upholstery, trying to suppress the little shivers of anticipation that ran up her spine. Nicholas got in and started the car.

Really, thought Tansy, as they turned into Ascot Avenue, I could almost have walked!

She had said very little during the three-minute drive. Nicholas had talked briefly about a large cheque that had been presented to the children's ward, and how they had coerced him into accepting it formally, and being photographed by the local paper.

Tansy made appropriate comments, but felt unnaturally tongue-tied. Her fingers tightly gripped her grey leather shoulder-bag. It had been a long time since she had accepted a dinner invitation. She'd almost forgotten what it was like.

Nicholas steered the car smoothly up a wide drive which curved in front of a large white house with an imposing Doric-style entrance. Tansy felt relieved that he hadn't seen her tiny flat, cosy as it was.

'Here we are.' He turned to her. 'Hungry?'

'Don't tell me you've cooked the meal!' she said jokingly.

'No, not tonight. Beth is a much better cook than I.'

As they approached the house, he turned to her. 'Beth had to go out tonight, unfortunately, but she won't be long. I wonder if——' He glanced around him. 'No, she hasn't gone yet, her car's still there. And she wouldn't have gone while I was away.'

Tansy was feeling bemused as he opened the front door. Why shouldn't Beth go out at the same time as himself? The door opened on to a large square hall, carpeted in dark blue and relieved with white paintwork and a pale blue and grey wallpaper. Nicholas took Tansy's coat and ushered her into a room on the right of the curving staircase.

'I'll just go and have a word with Beth,' he told her, smiling. 'Make yourself at home.'

Tansy walked slowly across the deep-pile carpet, noticing the expensive oak furniture, the heavy gold velvet curtains, the collection of books on the shelves, the framed photographs on a bureau. She went closer. One was of a rather plain youngish woman with a pretty dark-haired child. Neither of them resembled Nicholas. A close friend? Beth? She put it back quickly as the door opened.

'Hello.'

With a vision of plump, middle-aged Beth on her mind, Tansy was surprised to see a child in a blue dressing-gown, a little dark-haired girl with incredibly deep blue eyes, almost purple. Like pansies, she thought irrelevantly. And at the same moment she recognised the child in the photograph, now perhaps a couple of years older.

'Hello,' she smiled.

The child plumped herself into one of the beige-and-gold armchairs and stared at Tansy.

'Are you from the hospital?' she asked.

'Yes, I'm a doctor.'

'Do you look after children?'

'Yes.'

'I thought as much,' said the child solemnly. 'What's your name?'

'Dr Blair.'

'What's your first name? Mine's Gemma.'

'Tansy. And now you know both my names, so you must tell me yours.' She sat opposite.

Gemma laughed. '*You* know!'

'How can I? I've never met you before.'

Gemma looked slyly at her. 'Gemma Rosemary!' And she laughed hilariously.

'That's very nice,' said Tansy.

It was becoming a distinct possibility to Tansy that Gemma was Beth's daughter, and that meant she would have to revise her assumption about Beth's being middle-aged. Gemma appeared to be about five or six, which meant Beth was probably only in her thirties, or even younger. Tansy felt a sudden stab of jealousy. Supposing Beth was very young and very attractive? And she was living here, seeing Nicholas every day——

'Were you looking at the photographs?' asked Gemma, still watching Tansy in a most disconcerting way.

'I looked at one of you, when you were younger.'

'Oh, that one! I was little then.'

Tansy hid a smile. 'Yes, I could see that. And is the lady with you your mother?'

A shutter seemed to come across Gemma's face. She jumped from the chair and ran across to the bureau.

'I haven't got a mother! A little girl killed her!' She grabbed the photograph and thrust it behind a cushion. Tansy was shocked. Was the woman in the picture her mother? Was it Beth? If so, she wasn't particularly attractive, or even very young. Perhaps Beth didn't pose the threat she had imagined. So why was Gemma threatened by her? All her training told her the child was bothered by something. Did she resent her mother? Did she wish she were dead?

'Of course, you're much bigger now,' said Tansy, attempting to defuse the tense atmosphere.

Gemma turned to look at her. 'Of course I am. I'm six now—I had a birthday last week. How old are you?'

Gemma, that isn't the sort of question you ask grown-up visitors,' came a voice from the doorway, and Nicholas strode into the room, pushing the door behind him.

'Sorry, Daddy,' said Gemma, showing no contrition. But Tansy hardly noticed this. She was staring at Nicholas, her voice suddenly paralysed, a heavy weight in her stomach.

Daddy. Nicholas was Gemma's father. And if Beth was her mother—— Why hadn't he told her this? Why had he invited her to dinner, and dinner without Beth, of all things? Yet he hadn't kept Beth secret. He'd been very open about it. Why had he brought her here?

'Nicholas——' she began, getting up from her chair.

'I see Gemma has already introduced herself,' he said cheerfully, oblivious to her discomfiture.

'Yes——'

'And if I know her, she's already found out your name, your job, your family.'

Tansy smiled wanly. 'Almost.'

'Don't you think she'd make a good psychiatrist?' he continued. Tansy was dumbfounded by his casual attitude. She fidgeted in her chair.

'Nicholas, I don't think——' she began.

'Beth has just gone. She wanted to come and meet you, but she'd promised to be early. You'll like Beth, Tansy.'

Tansy couldn't believe her ears. But, before she could reply, Gemma ran to him and he picked her up, kissing her soft cheek.

'If she's gone, Daddy,' she whispered, 'may I stay up with you for a while?'

'You little slyboots,' he murmured, tugging a lock of black curly hair.

'It's only seven o'clock,' the child protested. 'I can tell the time now. And you promised, Daddy! You said when I was six I could stay up till half-past seven!'

'But not tonight, darling. I have a guest.'

'I won't be a nuisance—honestly! I'll be ever so good. I have been good, haven't I, Tansy?'

'Dr Tansy,' said Nicholas automatically.

'I'm sure you have,' said Tansy diplomatically. 'But I'm only a visitor, it isn't for me to say. Did you say you can tell the time? Then I expect you can read, can't you?'

Gemma wriggled to the floor and looked indignantly up at Tansy.

'I could read when I was four! Mummy taught me.'

A strange look passed across Nicholas's face which Tansy didn't miss. She kneeled to be on Gemma's level.

'Then why don't you read for a while in your room, then at half-past seven your—daddy—will come and put you to bed.'

'I'm not a baby! I can put myself to bed!'

'Then he can come and tuck you in. I promise.'

Gemma surveyed her seriously for a moment.

'Will you come and kiss me goodnight, Dr Tansy?'

There was a sudden wrenching at Tansy's heart. She tweaked Gemma's nose.

'Of course I will, if you want me to.'

'Then I'm going to bed now. I've had a busy day.' At the door Gemma turned, and still in a grown-up voice, she said, 'I don't like chicken supreme, anyway.' She put on a haughty look, and they heard her running lightly up the stairs.

Tansy and Nicholas looked at each other, and, in spite of herself, Tansy laughed.

'She's a poppet, your daughter,' she said quietly, a lump in her throat.'

'She is, isn't she?' He came and sat in the chair Gemma had vacated. Tansy remained standing.

'Why didn't you tell me about her?' she asked.

'Because—oh, hell, does it matter?'

'If I'd known of her existence I don't think I'd have come here tonight.'

He leaned forward, looking puzzled. 'Why should Gemma put you off coming to dinner?'

'Are you just being obtuse, Nicholas? Isn't it obvious? You have a child; a child usually has a mother—in other words, your wife. It was very cruel to invite me here under false pretences—unless, of course, you had another motive for inviting me.'

He looked rather shamefaced, then he nodded. 'Can we discuss it later? Because first——'

'This wasn't meant to be just a social occasion?'

'Well, yes—and no. Look——'

'Did you deliberately invite me tonight because your wife would be out?' Tansy demanded.

Nicholas stood up and took her hand. 'I'm afraid I forgot you've not long been here at Greenstead, so obviously you haven't heard. Sit down, Tansy. Let me explain.'

Even through her anger, Tansy was acutely aware of the firm, warm pressure of his fingers. And there was that look again in his eyes, the expression she had misunderstood. He released her hand and they sat opposite each other.

'Of course Gemma had a mother,' he said slowly.

'Had?' she queried.

'Gemma's mother died almost a year ago.'

So the child had told the truth, thought Tansy immediately. But—a little girl killed her? What had she meant? Could Mrs Vernon have died in childbirth? Unusual these days, but possible.

'I'm afraid I jumped to conclusions,' she admitted. 'I'm always doing it. Not in my job, of course—that would be fatal. But I assumed Beth——'

'You thought Beth was Gemma's mother?'

'A natural assumption. I saw the photograph, a woman with her arm around Gemma.'

Nicholas's gaze raked the row of photographs. 'Which one?'

'Gemma hid it behind a cushion, for some reason. This one.' She retrieved the photograph in its wooden frame. Nicholas took it. He stared at it for a long time.

'You thought this was Beth?'

'Naturally.'

'This was Gemma's mother—June.' He spoke very quietly, with a break in his voice. Tansy felt embarrassed. She felt she was intruding on his grief. A year wasn't long, and he must have loved her deeply.

'They aren't alike,' she said, to ease her disquiet. He didn't answer. He replaced the photograph on the bureau, his back turned to Tansy.

'I'm sorry,' she whispered. He turned suddenly.

'Why should you be? It's my fault, I should have told you before. Now I've invited you to dinner, so dinner you shall have.' Forced gaiety was in his voice and his smile, and Tansy stifled the urge to kiss away his hurt.

'Besides, it's chicken supreme,' she said brightly, and he laughed.

'That child of mine always lets the cat out of the bag! Come on. Beth left it all ready in the trolley.'

It seemed so natural to take his hand as they crossed the wide hall to the dining-room, as attractive as the other room, with muted pink walls and a deep rose carpet. The heavy grey curtains were drawn across the tall windows, and the black ash table had been laid with white damask and silver cutlery. Tansy couldn't help wondering how Nicholas had acquired such wealth, since, as a fairly new paediatric consultant, it would normally have taken a number of years to aspire to this type of house and furnishings.

But these thoughts soon left her mind when he set before her a dish of assorted melon, decorated with slices of strawberry, and she realised she was hungry.

As she ate she realised she had almost made a fool of herself again. Beth probably was plump and middle-aged, after all. And Nicholas was as likely as not completely uninterested in her as anything other than a housekeeper. Tansy smiled to herself and took another spoonful of the delicious melon.

'Do you come from Wiltshire?' asked Nicholas politely.

'No. I was born in Lincolnshire, then, when my father died, my mother and I moved to Wiltshire—Marlborough.'

'Your mother is still there?'

'She married again, an American called Ted. They went to live in the States—oh, must be five or six years ago.'

She was aware that she had deliberately faked an air of indifference. Was it to fool Nicholas or herself into believing she didn't really care about her mother's departure? She smiled brightly at him and swallowed her last piece of melon.

'Mmm—that was delicious. Beth is a good cook.'

'Beth is good at everything.'

She glanced sharply at him, but he was manoeuvring a slice of strawberry on to his spoon. His voice was a little muffled as he said, 'I suppose you've left a few disappointed suitors wherever you've come from.'

Tansy studied the discreet pattern in the damask tablecloth, and traced it with her finger before answering casually, 'No, I've not left anyone behind. No one at all.'

'Why did you leave your last hospital? Or shouldn't I ask?'

'I just wanted a change. Doesn't everyone? And how long have you been at Greenstead?'

'Four years. I left Winchester because there was a junior consultant's post going here in Swindon.'

'Royal Hampshire? St Paul's?' Tansy queried.

His eyes widened. 'You were at Winchester? I was at the Royal.'

'So was I. I worked my house year there, and there was a chance of staying on, so I took it. I must have started there as you left.'

He nodded. 'That seems very likely.' He stared at her

for a moment, then got up, collecting the dishes. 'I'll fetch the chicken.'

Tansy sat back in her chair. It was turning out to be quite an interesting evening. As long as he didn't become too interested in her! Fancy his being at Winchester! He must have been living there when she was a medical student at Southampton University. He might even have been around when she met Rod. Rod had just started a surgical house job at Southampton. She had been drawn to him from the first moment she saw him. She had always loved the way his nose crinkled when he laughed—and he'd laughed a lot! She still felt the same pain of loss when she remembered that day, the last time she saw him. That dreadful day. Had she really lost him long before that? And she had made a vow then that no man would take advantage of her feelings again.

Miles away, she didn't realise Nicholas had returned until a plate was placed in front of her; steaming rice surrounding chunks of firm white chicken in a creamy sauce with shreds of red pepper. It smelled wonderful, and it tasted just as good. Beth certainly was a good cook.

They ate silently. Nicholas seemed to be thinking. Finally he said, 'What did you think of Gemma?'

'She's a lovely child. You must be proud of her. And——' she glanced at her watch '—do you realise it's half-past seven?'

'Oh, lord!' He jumped up, and Tansy followed.

'I promised too,' she reminded him, and followed him up the wide stairs.

Gemma seemed to be asleep already, her dark hair tumbled on the pillow with its pattern of red rosebuds, like the duvet. Tansy, suddenly nervous, held back as Nicholas gently tucked in the child's arm. Gemma opened her eyes and lifted her arms to hug him. Then she saw Tansy.

'Kiss,' she demanded sleepily. Tansy bent over her. She was conscious of Nicholas's proximity, and her heart was pounding. Gemma smelled of baby powder. Tansy

kissed the soft, velvety cheek, and the little girl closed
her eyes and snuggled down. She looked so very vulnerable. For a moment Tansy recalled the moment in the
sitting-room, when Gemma had snatched the photograph
from the shelf and hidden it. It was a disturbing memory.
And Tansy couldn't help wondering about June, and
how she had died. And why she had died.

Nicholas switched out the light, and they crept
downstairs.

'I think it's about time we finished our meal,' he said,
resting his hand on her shoulder. Tansy quivered inside
at the shock that ran through her.

'There's more?' she asked.

'Lots more,' he said quietly. She resumed her seat,
and was served with a delicious concoction of bananas
and coconut in a warm caramel sauce, decorated with a
whirl of cream and a slice of mandarin orange.

'We'll have coffee in here,' he said, when they had
finished, taking her back to the sitting-room. 'And what
about some soft music?'

He put on a tape, and soon the light haunting sounds
of 'Morning' from *Peer Gynt* filled the room. He drew
the curtains, switching on two small wall lights which
cast soft shadows over everything. Against her will,
Tansy felt excited. Surely he had intended her to feel
relaxed? She lay back and closed her eyes. The chink of
cups roused her, and Nicholas stood watching her.
Flushing, she hurriedly sat up.

'I'm so sorry—I didn't mean to nod off——'

'Don't apologise. I expect you've had a busy day. I
couldn't help looking at you, you looked so peaceful. Do
you know what I thought?'

Tansy shook her head. He sat on the arm of the chair.

'I wished I were Gemma—or, at least, her age.
Children have no inhibitions, they say what they feel.
She wanted you to kiss her, so she asked you.'

Tansy tensed. There was a roaring in her ears. She
was afraid to look into those grey eyes, afraid to see what
they might show. Nicholas came and sat next to her on

the sofa. She tried to detach herself, tried to concentrate on the music, 'Anitra's Dance'.

'If I ask you to kiss me, Tansy, will you?' he whispered. She could heardly breathe. She felt she was losing control.

'You have to ask first,' she said breathlessly.

'Kiss,' he said, in a low voice, and before she could reply, his arms had taken her, his lips came down on hers, and it seemed the world had stopped, and all the stars had crowded in behind her eyes. She knew she was responding, but she couldn't help it.

Then he released her and looked at her, and she could see desire in his eyes. She began to panic. This wasn't supposed to happen! She should have resisted more, should have refused. Now he'd think all the wrong things about her. The panic must have shown in her eyes, because he got up and began to pour the coffee.

'I'm sorry,' he said shakily. 'I didn't intend that to happen.'

'It doesn't matter.' Her lips still felt the pressure of his.

'You're right, it doesn't matter. After all, what's in a kiss?'

'Everyone kisses these days,' agreed Tansy in a similar light tone. 'Kisses don't mean anything. Just forget it happened. There's no need to apologise.'

'If that's what you want,' Nicholas said quietly. 'Sugar?'

'One, please.'

He sat in another chair, and they began to discuss music and politics and medicine. In fact, anything that had nothing to do with romance, and couples, and physical contact. Nicholas's smile was wooden; Tansy's laugh was forced and brittle. Inside, she felt hollow and bereft. It had started out so well—if you didn't count the earlier misunderstanding over June. Now it was all ruined, all because she was stupidly afraid to admit to her true feelings. She might as well go home.

As she started to rise, the front door opened and closed, and footsteps hurried up the stairs.

'Beth's come back,' said Nicholas, obviously relieved.

'Perhaps I'd better go,' said Tansy. 'It's getting late.'

He glanced at the clock, but didn't seem to notice it was only just after ten. He leaned forward.

'Actually, Tansy,' he began, and she tensed in her seat, 'I told a bit of a fib when I came to fetch you tonight.'

'Did you?'

'I implied that this was a purely social occasion. And now I feel pretty awful about what I'm going to ask you.' He was watching her closely.

'It wasn't meant to be a social occasion?' she echoed. 'I'm afraid I don't understand.'

'I invited you here because I need your professional advice. About Gemma.'

Tansy wasn't sure how to answer. She remembered his insistence that she came early. Was that a deliberate ploy so that she could see Gemma before the child went to bed? Why hadn't she suspected anything? And now she was remembering something else he had said. He had his own reasons for wanting her to come early. And she'd been so dazed she hadn't thought to ask him what those reasons were. He was looking intently at her, waiting for her response.

'You've talked to her,' he said at last. 'What did you think? Does she seem normal for a six-year-old? Or disturbed? That's why I had to let you meet her. Because I'm very worried about her.'

CHAPTER FOUR

CONFLICTING thoughts raced around Tansy's head. Nicholas had deceived her. Like Rod, he had deceived her. Gemma—disturbed. Worried about her.

She wasn't sure whether she should feel angry or concerned. Of course she felt angry. He had used her. But his anxiety about Gemma was genuine enough, she could see it in his eyes, and it temporarily displaced her anger to a degree. Was Gemma disturbed?

'I hardly know her, Nicholas. We talked for no more than five minutes, and that isn't long enough to reach a decision——'

'She hid the photograph,' he interrupted. 'Didn't you think that was strange?'

'Certainly a little odd. But she seemed normal enough the rest of the time. She seems outgoing and friendly. You recall she asked me, a stranger, to kiss her goodnight.'

The memory of that other kiss then threatened to overwhelm her, and her previous anger returned with vigour. She stood up.

'Nicholas, it's no use my pretending all this—this deceit doesn't matter. You've——'

Nicholas leapt to his feet.

'Deceit? I don't——'

'Yes, deceit!' Spots of colour burned in Tansy's cheeks. 'You brought me here, to your house, on the pretence that you liked me, wanted my company, wanted to share a meal with me—for all I know, you probably just felt sorry for me——' She knew she was saying all the wrong things, but she couldn't stop.

'Tansy, I didn't——'

'Oh, yes, you've admitted it to me now. It wasn't my company you wanted, but my professional expertise. I'm not surprised you felt ashamed at taking advantage of me. It wasn't part of the deal, was it?'

She was finding it hard to ignore the hurt and puzzlement in his soft grey eyes.

'Listen, Tansy——'

'I just don't understand why you couldn't have been honest about it all, instead of arranging all this—hospitality, assignation, tête-à-tête, call it what you like. I'm sorry, Nicholas, I feel I've been used, and I'd like to go home.' He reached out and took her arm, but she moved to shake it off. 'Don't worry, I can walk. It's not far.'

His grip tightened. 'Tansy, you've got it all wrong. Let me explain——'

'I thought you had? Surely you brought me here quite simply to act as unofficial psychiatrist for your daughter?'

'I admit it looks like that. I've gone about it in the wrong way.' Nicholas's voice sounded sad, and she glanced sharply at him.

'I'm sorry too,' she said firmly. 'That's how it seemed to me. Thank you for the meal, Nicholas, it was very nice, and I enjoyed meeting Gemma.'

Suddenly she couldn't meet his gaze. Was she turning her back on a child's need? Nicholas must have sensed her indecision, because he pulled her towards him. She was only inches away from him and she could smell his spicy aftershave. Her heart was racing.

'I know you like Gemma,' he said softly. 'So can we start all over again? Will you help her?'

Impulsively, Tansy turned away from him. She felt she was losing control, and that hadn't happened in a long time.

'You've put me in a difficult position, Nicholas,' she said quietly. 'I feel very angry, I don't like being used.'

'I understand that, Tansy, and it wasn't meant. I'm sorry.'

'Gemma's a sweet child, and I'd be a poor doctor if I turned my back on a child that needed help.' She turned to look at him. 'It's Gemma I'm thinking of, you understand.'

'Naturally.' Why did his grey eyes seem to search her face when she spoke? Was she really so transparent that her true thoughts showed?

'I think you'd better tell me, then, why you're so worried about her,' she went on.

'Shall we sit down?' said Nicholas.

She moved quickly away from him. Yet everything in her was rebelling against her show of icy frigidity. But it would be too risky to give in. So she sat on a chair while he sat on the sofa almost opposite.

'My first question has to be, do you think it has anything to do with her mother's death?' she told him.

Nicholas frowned. 'I didn't think so, but I feel now it's a distinct possibility.'

'Was she very upset when she died?'

'Not as upset as I expected. She was very shocked, like a little ghost for a long time—hardly spoke. But I never saw her cry. And she never mentioned her.'

'Did you feel this was natural?'

'How was I to know? Children react to a parent's death in so many different ways. I suppose I did wish she'd talk about it. Yet we didn't like to mention it in case it did upset her once she'd got over it. She didn't mention it to anyone.'

Tansy nodded. 'But you say her behaviour has changed too.'

'She's become destructive, defiant, easily upset. Not all the time, you understand. Just now and again.'

'Has anyone else remarked on it? Her teacher, for example?' asked Tansy.

'Her teacher's quite new, so she doesn't know what Gemma was like before. But yes, she has mentioned that Gemma gets upset over little things—loses her temper.'

'Anyone else? Beth, for instance? Has she been with you long?'

A strange expression flitted across Nicholas's face. 'She came here just before June died,' he said.

'When June was ill, you mean?' queried Tansy.

'June wasn't really ill. She thought she was. Her death was very unexpected.'

'So it had to be a great shock to Gemma. I'm not surprised she's having problems. A child of five doesn't always understand the meaning of death.'

Nicholas leaned forward and looked into her eyes. 'Did you feel she's disturbed?' he asked earnestly.

Tansy's heart fluttered as she replied. 'She acted a little strangely over the photograph. Impossible to know how deep it goes unless I talk to her again. It may just be a simple misunderstanding on her part.'

'Will you come here to see her?'

The temptation to agree was strong. 'I don't think that would be advisable—at least, not at the beginning. I have all the necessary equipment and materials at the hospital. It's not just a matter of talking, you see, not with children. You have to gain their confidence, let them play, and talk to you as they play. They don't understand their feelings when they're very young—they can't put them into words. The way they play tells you a lot.'

'I do understand,' said Nicholas. 'I'm a paediatrician. When can you see her?'

Tansy hesitated. 'I wish you'd asked Dan Rice first. Oh, don't get me wrong, I'm quite happy to do it. But if I find she needs more sessions with me, I think I ought to tell him what I'm doing. You do see that?'

'Naturally. I suppose he'll want it all made official.'

'He may. Would you agree to that?'

'I had hoped to avoid her problem being put on hospital records,' Nicholas confessed. 'Perhaps I ought to have a word with Dan myself.'

'He may wonder why you didn't approach him in the first place. After all, he is the chief,' said Tansy.

'And if I say I think it needs a woman's touch?' He grinned, and she found herself smiling back.

'I hope he'll believe you!'

'So when can you see her?'

'The only time I can give her tomorrow is four-thirty—a cancellation.'

Nicholas looked anxious. 'Tomorrow—Thursday. I'm not sure. Beth could bring her, but she has an evening class at six, so she won't be able to stay. I don't suppose——' He cast her an appealing glance, and she knew whatever he was going to ask, she would be unable to refuse him.

'Could Gemma stay with you until I arrive? If you have a later patient, could she play somewhere, in another room?'

Another room. For a brief moment Tansy saw herself in another room, a small white room with dark green curtains. She was standing at the window that looked out on to a park where children played on the swings and slides and roundabouts, while their mothers watched indulgently. The door behind her had opened, and she knew it was time. And she was afraid to turn round, afraid she'd lose control. . .

'Perhaps one of the nurses would keep an eye on her?' Nicholas was saying. She jerked back to reality, to the beautiful beige and gold room, with the heavy velvet curtains.

'Oh, there'll be no need for that,' she assured him. 'She'll be my last patient. I'll keep her with me until you arrive. We can play games.'

'She likes you,' said Nicholas, smiling.

'She's a child. I'd like to help her.'

Nicholas rose and moved towards her. Catching her breath, she stood and straightened her skirt.

'I think I'd better go now, if you don't mind.'

Tansy passed a weary hand across her brow and closed the last file. Caroline Porter, a nine-year-old with severe anxiety, had timidly waved from the doorway, her first gesture of friendliness, and Tansy had felt quite buoyed up inside. But it was taking such a long time, even with Hattie's help.

She glanced at the clock on the wall. Four-forty. She'd

kept Gemma waiting. She'd tried to keep to her allotted time, but Mrs Porter, an over-anxious mother herself, had insisted on telling Tansy in great detail Caroline's last three dreams.

Tansy had dreamed too, last night. And in her dream, too, the strangest things had happened. First she had been in the room with green curtains with Rod, then Nicholas had come in with a girl dressed as a bride, but she couldn't see her face because of the thick white veil. Then Nicholas had changed into Rod, and even her mother had been there, on the arm of Daniel Rice. And as the curtains had changed to gold velvet, Rod had called her and she'd woken up. Totally confusing, and obviously a result of what had happened the evening before.

Nicholas had driven her home and, as she had reached to open the car door, he had turned her towards him and kissed her again. Not a deep, passionate kiss like the one earlier, but a soft, tender kiss that barely brushed her lips, yet left her feeling even more disturbed than before.

'Thank you,' he had said softly, touching her cheek with his finger. Tansy was glad he couldn't see her expression in the dark.

'Thank you—for the lovely meal.'

'I'm sorry if my behaviour wasn't up to scratch.'

She stared at him, but his face was in shadow. Was he smiling?

'You don't have to apologise.' She spoke stiffly. She didn't want him referring to the incident. She had meant to be resolute, not show her feelings. She would rather forget it.

'But I do. I invited you for a meal——'

'A consultation.' Her retort was spontaneous.

'You're very prickly about it, aren't you? Won't you let me explain?'

She reached across again to the door-handle, but again he turned her to face him, and his grip was strong on her arms.

'I thought you had.'

He didn't answer for a moment. 'Don't you like me, Tansy?'

'I—of course I like you. Look, we've been through all this before. This evening was arranged so I could see Gemma——'

'Partly.' His hand rested on hers. It was warm and somehow comforting. 'But mostly because I wanted to know you better. There's something strange about you, Tansy. You only seem to come alive when you're discussing your work.'

'I don't think——'

His strong fingers grasped hers.

'The rest of the time, you seem to shut people out. Why?'

Tansy laughed shakily. 'I think you're imagining things. If I shut people out I wouldn't have come to your house tonight.'

'You've turned down everyone else.'

She gasped. 'You've been prying into my private life! How dare you?' She wrenched herself away from him.

'No, I haven't, Tansy. You know what hospitals are like—the grapevine. You're quite new, so naturally everyone talks about you for a while, tries to find out what makes you tick. It'll die down.'

'And what do they say about me?' She spoke through tight lips.

'I don't think it's important. I don't believe them, anyway. Not after the way you kissed me——'

'Excuse me!' she retorted. 'It was you who did the kissing. Now, if you don't mind, I have things to do before I go to bed.'

Nicholas gave a long dramatic sigh. 'All right. I'm sorry you feel like this. If it's just a professional relationship you want, then it's a pity, because I shan't give up. If you insist on putting up barriers, I can't promise I shan't try to break them down. It's up to you now.'

He started up the car. Tansy sat very still.

'Goodnight, Tansy. See you tomorrow when I collect Gemma.'

She couldn't help feeling like a naughty schoolgirl, called to see the Head. She climbed out of the car.

'Goodnight.' But Nicholas was already moving away. A small shiver of anticipation ran through her as she watched his car disappear. Up to her now. He'd stated his intentions; she'd tried to state hers. But they weren't quite as clear-cut as that. She felt a bit like Jekyll and Hyde. Yet she was still determined to deny that other side of her. And suddenly it made her feel sad.

Sighing, because tonight could have been something really good, if she'd let it, she unlocked the front door and let herself into the house.

And now, in spite of trying not to think about Nicholas, her pulses were racing because in about an hour he would be coming to collect Gemma. She pressed the buzzer on her desk. Soon Beth and Gemma would be coming through the door. At last she would see what Beth looked like, the legendary Beth who seemed to be a genius at everything.

The door opened, and Pamela came in, holding the hand of a solemn-faced Gemma. Tansy must have looked surprised, because the receptionist explained, 'Dr Vernon brought her—said her name's Gemma. He asked me to keep an eye on her until you were ready. Something about a change of plan—he said you'd know what that meant. I must say, she's been very good, haven't you?'

But Gemma was staring at Tansy with astonishment. 'Dr Tansy!' she exclaimed. 'You came to see me last night!'

'That's right,' said Tansy, 'I did.'

'Is she a patient?' asked Pamela curiously. 'Dr Vernon didn't say anything, just left her here.'

'Er—not really. I'm—sort of—babysitting for an hour or so.'

Pamela stared at her, then at Gemma. 'Of course! I thought I'd seen her before. At the Spring Fête, wasn't it? She's Dr Vernon's little girl, isn't she? When I saw her I said to Elizabeth, is this another of Dr Tansy's children? I haven't seen her before. Then Elizabeth said she thought she looked familiar, and I sort of remembered, then. I thought she was a patient, but when Dr Vernon didn't say anything I just assumed you'd be sure to know about it, probably made out the notes yourself——'

'What did you say, Pamela? To Elizabeth?' Tansy interrupted.

'What? Oh—Dr Tansy's children! That's what we call them, your patients. Tansy's children. They all love you so much. They never want to leave you.'

'I see.' Tansy's voice was sharp. 'Well, you'd better get back, in case——'

'Caroline was last, Dr Blair. If you remember, Darren James cancelled—rehearsal for a school play. That's why I thought Gemma had come, to fill the cancellation——'

'I'm just looking after her for a while. Thank you, Pamela.'

'Yes, I see. Look, I'm sorry, Dr Blair, if I offended you, calling your patients Tansy's children. I didn't mean to be familiar, but we all call them that, it's a compliment, really——'

'Yes, you're right.' Tansy realised she was being oversensitive, and smiled at the young receptionist. 'I'll take Gemma now.'

Pamela patted the child on the head and went back to clear up the office. Tansy took Gemma's hand. It felt soft and trusting.

'Am I a patient?' Gemma asked, as Tansy closed the door behind them.

'What makes you ask that?' Tansy was unsure of what Nicholas had told his daughter.

'Well, this is a hospital, and when people go to see doctors it's because they're ill, so they're patients. Daddy told me that.'

'But you're not ill, are you?' Tansy crossed to a small table where there was a pile of modelling clay. Gemma followed her.

'I was sick on my birthday because I ate too much trifle,' said Gemma seriously.

Tansy smiled. 'I'm sure you're better now.'

'Mummy wasn't ill, but she came here to see doctors. Was it because they were friends, like you?'

'Am I your friend?' asked Tansy gently.

'Daddy said so.'

Tansy felt a warm glow inside. Nicholas's friend. Or should she take it literally, as Gemma had stated it— Gemma's friend? Either way, it felt nice.

'Your mummy wasn't ill, yet she came to see someone here?' she probed gently. 'Who did she come to see?'

'Dr Whittaker. And Dr Spencer.'

Tansy digested this carefully. Al Whittaker was a neurologist. Flora Spencer was a psychiatrist. What was the connection? A suspected brain disease that was really psychological? Or vice versa? It all depended on which consultant June saw first. And, recalling what Nicholas had said about June's sudden death, Tansy thought it pointed to something like a brain tumour, or a sub-arachnoid haemorrhage, due to congenital weakness of an artery in the brain. Tansy nodded. It all fitted— June's age, the suddenness of her death. Could she have been having headaches before it happened?

All this reasoning took only seconds to pass through Tansy's mind. She glanced at Gemma, who was standing at the table, fingering a lump of pink modelling clay.

'Why don't you sit down, Gemma?' she suggested. 'Would you like to make something for me?'

Gemma sat in a little plastic chair, and Tansy kneeled on the carpet beside her.

'Why is your name Tansy?' Gemma asked suddenly, kneading the clay.

'I don't know. I suppose my mother liked flowers. Tansy's a flower rather like a big yellow daisy.'

'Your hair's like a yellow daisy,' remarked the child.

'Yes, I suppose it is.'

'I wish I were blonde,' Gemma added. 'Katie Brown is blonde.'

'Is Katie Brown your friend?'

'She's my best friend—sometimes. She's ever so clever, she comes top in nearly everything, except painting. Miss Fletcher made her the Fairy Queen in the pantomime last Christmas. That's because she's blonde.'

'Were you in the pantomime?' asked Tansy.

'I was Snow White. I'd rather have been the Fairy Queen.' The clay was taking the shape of a person.

'I expect you made a lovely Snow White. You have just the right hair for it.'

Tansy gently touched the thick, springy curls, but Gemma jerked away impatiently.

'I'd rather be blonde.'

'Didn't you like being Snow White?'

'Don't you know what she did? The wicked Queen brought her a poisoned apple, and Snow White ate it! I wouldn't have done that!'

'Perhaps she thought she was just an old woman,' suggested Tansy.

Gemma angrily fixed a pointed hat on the model's head. 'Somebody must have told her not to take things from strangers. My mummy told me——'

She tightened her lips and crushed the clay figure, then flattened it on the table.

'What did your mummy tell you?' prompted Tansy gently.

'Sweets from strangers can kill! Didn't you know that?'

This was an unusual interpretation of the warning. Wasn't it the giver of the sweets who could be dangerous? Gemma was rolling another ball of clay around the table.

'Can you make me an elephant?' asked Tansy. 'I like elephants.'

'All right.' Gemma's small chubby fingers quickly formed the body and the legs.

'Do you like school?' asked Tansy.

'Sometimes. I like singing and dancing. And painting.' Gemma rolled the clay into a long thin worm.

'What do you like to paint?'

'We paint houses, and gardens, and flowers. Things like that.'

The trunk was in place; now for the ears. Tansy was aware her question hadn't been answered. And so far there had been little real sign of Gemma's disturbance. She reached out and rolled a piece of blue clay on the table.

'Daddy took me to the pantomime,' said Gemma, without prompting. 'We saw *Aladdin*.'

'Did your mummy go too?' asked Tansy.

'She didn't feel well. She had a headache.'

'And did Beth stay with her?'

'She hadn't come from America then.' Was Beth American? thought Tansy. Nicholas hadn't said so. But why should he?

'Did you ever go to the zoo with your mummy?' she probed gently.

Gemma walked the red elephant across the table on its little fat legs. She didn't answer, and Tansy felt a tingling inside.

'Didn't she take you to see the elephants?'

Gemma walked the elephant back, then pulled off its trunk and ears and poked a hole in its middle.

'Did you know snakes are poisonous?' she asked, rolling the remains of the elephant into a long red rope and pulling it across the table.

'This is a snake—it's got fangs. It'll kill you!' She thrust the 'head' of the snake at Tansy's arm. Tansy jumped, but forced herself to remain unshaken. The gesture had been unsettling, but in no way could she let Gemma see how she felt.

'You saw snakes at the zoo?' she asked, watching Gemma carefully.

Gemma wrapped the clay snake around her arm.

'Snakes can kill rabbits. I heard Daddy say my mummy was a rabbit.' Tansy was sure all this disturbing talk meant something vital. But it was difficult trying to work it out. There seemed such a lot of symbolism.

'She looked like a rabbit, you mean?' More like a pudding, on the photograph.

'I don't know. Do I look like a snake?' Gemma waved her hand in the air and the clay rope fell to the table. What's she trying to tell me? thought Tansy.

'You don't look a bit like a snake,' she smiled. 'You're much too pretty. You look just like Snow White.'

At that, Gemma's pretty face contorted, and she bared her teeth angrily.

'I'm not Snow White! I can't be Snow White! My mummy was Snow White!' She jumped from the table and ran around the room, knocking toys to the floor, tugging at the curtains.

'I'm the Wicked Witch! I'm the Wicked Witch!' The words, screamed at first, quickly disintegrated into tearful whispers. As she approached Tansy, the doctor reached out and drew her close. At first Gemma fought, hitting at her with her fists, then she collapsed against her, whispering, 'Wicked Witch! Wicked Witch!'

Tansy held her tightly, stroking her dark hair and making soothing noises. Outwardly calm, inside she felt exultant. The first breaking of the barriers had started.

She wiped Gemma's face, held a tissue while she blew her nose, dried the tears on her long eyelashes. Gemma relaxed against her, and her fingers curled around Tansy's neck.

Now would have been a good time to end the session. But there was no one here to take Gemma home, no mother to hug her and ask her if she'd had fun, to take her home and give her crumpets for tea by the fire. Tansy realised she was recalling her own happy childhood, and she felt acutely sorry for Gemma.

'I know,' she said. 'Wouldn't you like to paint me a picture?'

Gemma uncurled and looked at her. 'Anything I like?'

'Anything you like.'

'Only if you paint something too.'

'All right.'

Tansy knew she could never be described as an artist,

but she gamely attempted a blue vase of pink flowers, that didn't look like any flowers she could name. Occasionally she cast glances at Gemma's complicated painting, and was a little dismayed at the large amount of black.

Her tongue sticking out, Gemma added red and yellow, and Tansy wondered if it was meant to be a fire. But she said nothing, and laboriously painted pink petals that rather resembled discoloured bananas.

Finally Gemma put down her brush and wiped her hand on her cotton overall. Tansy moved over to admire it. She stood back to see better. A figure with a yellow face, wearing a red dress, appeared to be lying on the ground, asleep. Other figures, dressed in black, surrounded her, their hands on their faces. Crying? thought Tansy. Not all were in black, though. One of them, in yellow with a black hat, was standing in the corner, snowflakes falling from its hand, forming a snowy pool by the sleeping figure.

'She's dead,' said Gemma, pointing at the yellow-faced figure. 'She's dead. And she killed her.'

She snatched up the brush and rapidly painted red lines across the figure in yellow.

CHAPTER FIVE

THERE were so many questions Tansy wanted to ask, but the expression on Gemma's face stopped her. Gently she took the brush from the child's hand and washed it in the jar of water.

'I think you've been listening to too many fairy stories,' she said, smiling. 'Come and tell me about *Aladdin*.'

But Gemma remained staring at what she had created, as if unable to believe what she saw.

'What a pity you spoiled your picture,' said Tansy. 'Now you won't be able to show your daddy.'

'It wasn't for Daddy,' said Gemma. 'It was for you.' Impulsively, she pulled the painting from the easel and screwed it into a ball.

'Then wasn't it a good job I saw it before you destroyed it! What would you like to do now?'

'I want to go home.'

Sighing, Tansy glanced at her watch. Ten minutes past five. The time had gone quickly. Surely Nicholas would come soon? The familiar pounding of her heart began, the tightness in her chest. Trying to ignore it, she crossed to the cupboard where the family dolls were kept. The children always enjoyed playing with the dolls, and, often, it was the only way of finding out how they felt about things. She placed the furniture on the table, and the box of dolls.

'Do you like these, Gemma? Don't you think this one looks like you?' She held out a small one with black hair, dressed in pink.

Gemma took it, examined it, even its white knickers and socks, and sat it in an armchair. Interest had taken hold, and she searched the box for the others she wanted. First she took one with fair hair, dressed in blue. She considered it for a while, her nose crinkled up, and for a fleeting moment she reminded Tansy of—— Then she put it to one side.

'Not the mummy doll?' prompted Tansy.

'Not *her* mummy.' Gemma found a male doll in a grey suit and placed it next to the Gemma doll.

'That's Daddy.' It was obvious that Gemma adored her father, and the feeling was mutual. Looking at the deep blue eyes, like pansies, the pink and white soft skin and the attractive dark hair, Tansy thought it would be so easy to adore Gemma. And her throat ached painfully.

Gemma had found another doll, with black hair and a green spotted dress. She placed it next to the rejected blonde doll.

'Not the mummy doll?' asked Tansy, trying to analyse why she had selected two, only to reject them. Yet she hadn't put them back in the box with the others.

'She's not a *real* mummy.' Tansy hadn't expected it to be so complicated. All those other women in the background!

Gemma now triumphantly produced a brown-haired doll in a lilac dress, which she laid on the sofa.

'She's asleep,' she explained, glancing at Tansy. She sat back and looked at the little tableau—June asleep, Nicholas and Gemma sitting together. Was June asleep? thought Tansy. Or ill? Or dead? And where was Beth, the housekeeper?

'You haven't picked Beth yet,' she suggested. Gemma gave her a withering look.

'Of course I have. That's her!' She picked up the blonde doll and sat her roughly in another chair. Tansy stared at it. Blonde? It didn't fit in with her own image of Beth. A sudden pang shot through her. Had she been right all along? Was Beth young and attractive? Perhaps she wasn't a housekeeper at all, more like an au pair. And she was living in Nicholas's house, seeing him every day, cooking him his meals—cordon bleu meals—washing his clothes, ironing his shirts, his pyjamas. Did he wear pyjamas? An image of a naked Nicholas, draped in a towel, fresh from the shower, assailed her mind. She forced it away, and made herself concentrate on what Gemma was doing.

Gemma was looking for something, lifting and moving things, tutting impatiently as she searched. Finally she tipped some pebbly remnants of coloured chalk from a box and placed them on a toy table. Next, Daddy was removed from the scene, then Beth, and only Gemma remained with the sleeping June. The table with the chalk remnants was placed in front of June by the Gemma doll, which then walked away. The mummy doll then appeared to wake and eat the coloured chalk before lying down again. The Gemma doll returned and touched the June doll, then ran away. Finally, the daddy doll and the Beth doll removed the June doll, the daddy doll came back with the Gemma doll, and they hugged each other.

Was this the end of the story? thought Tansy. The story of June's demise? It seemed not. Beth was placed next to Daddy, followed by the Gemma doll squeezed between them.

Did Gemma resent the arrival of Beth? Did she want to keep Nicholas to herself now June had died? That scene with the pieces of chalk: Tansy tried to analyse it. If June hadn't been very ill before her death, was that medication she was taking?

Gemma now picked up the black-haired doll in the green dress and sat it next to the daddy doll. And that seemed to make her cross, and she tossed it into the box. A thought occurred to Tansy, an awful thought that jarred her. A dark-haired woman friend? The staff nurse she'd seen him with? An affair? She tightened her lips. It was nothing to do with her. Nicholas was a free agent.

She glanced at Gemma, who had all the dolls now seated at the table, even the dead mummy doll who was passing the daddy doll a cup of tea. Tansy smiled. Things were really starting to develop here.

The door opened. Gemma, absorbed, wasn't immediately aware of her father's presence until he spoke.

'Hi there.' His gaze met Tansy's, and she felt the colour rise in her cheeks. She looked away and pretended absorption in Gemma's play. Gemma jumped up, her eyes wide with happiness.

'Daddy!' She ran to him, and he picked her up and hugged her. Tansy turned away from them and began to tidy away the dolls.

'Are these meant to be flowers, poppet?' Nicholas asked Gemma.

Flushing, Tansy stood up and pulled the painting from the easel.

'It's mine, and I'm no artist.' She folded it roughly, and Nicholas looked amused.

'Did you paint anything, Gemma?' But his gaze was on Tansy, and she refused to meet it, refused to acknowledge the rapid beating of her heart.

'It wasn't very nice, Daddy. I screwed it up. Are we going home now?'

'Not just yet, poppet. I need to have a word with Dr Blair.'

'Dr Tansy, Daddy. Everyone calls her Dr Tansy.'

'Do they indeed? Well, how about you running along to the waiting-room and playing with the toys there? I shan't be long.'

'Can't I stay here?' begged Gemma. 'I shan't listen—I promise!'

Tansy laughed, and Nicholas tweaked the child's nose. 'Little pitchers have big ears,' he said. 'Run along. I saw jigsaw puzzles as I passed.'

'Oh, all right.' Gemma left the room and he closed the door, and Tansy couldn't stop the sudden racing inside herself.

'I can't stay long,' he said, perching himself on the corner of the desk. 'We have some friends coming from Oxford, and as Beth is out I have to be back before they arrive.'

His long, muscular, grey-trousered leg swung lazily. Tansy tore her gaze away and moved to the other side of the desk.

'Well, how did she do?' he went on.

'Perhaps you'd care to sit in the chair,' she suggested. 'I feel you're distracting me.'

'As you wish.' But his grey eyes twinkled, although his expression was serious, and for a moment she felt a yearning to go to him, to lie against his broad chest and pour out her troubles. Her heart pounded at the vision. The moment passed. She sat down. Nicholas followed suit, drawing his chair nearer to hers.

'She is disturbed,' said Tansy quietly. 'How seriously, I don't know. It seems to tie in with her mother's death, but it's quite possible it may be due to some misunderstanding.'

'Has she talked about it?' he asked.

'Not really. Children don't, Nicholas. Their actions reveal more than words. She's only six, but a bright child, articulate for her age. I'm quite confident we shall soon get to the bottom of it.'

'The sooner the better,' he said.

'Of course.' Tansy agreed automatically, but did she really mean it? As she saw it, she had a choice of two options. She could speed up the therapy, see less of Nicholas, and consequently reduce the chance of her feelings running away with her. Or she could drag it out to its utmost, savour every exquisitely painful moment of their meetings, torture herself. It was only infatuation, she knew, but infatuation could be as agonising as love while it lasted. And it was going to be almost impossible to hide it from him.

'Have you mentioned it to Dan Rice yet?' he asked.

'I shall, at the first opportunity.'

He nodded. 'What makes you feel it ties in with June's death?' His voice seemed curiously restrained.

'She called her Snow White, said Snow White had foolishly eaten the poisoned apple. I couldn't see the analogy then, but it made me wonder. Did June perhaps die of food poisoning?'

Nicholas smiled. He seemed relieved.

'No, it was nothing like that.'

'Yet she was ill beforehand, wasn't she?'

'No, not really ill. She thought she was.'

'You said that before,' said Tansy. 'But she came to see Al Whittaker and Flora Spencer. There must have been a reason, to see both of them.'

For a moment he looked angry. He stared hard at her. 'How did you know that?' he demanded.

'Gemma told me. Without any prompting, I can assure you.'

He drummed his fingers on the desk. 'She thought she had a serious disease, so it had to be checked out.'

'The disease didn't kill her?'

'No. Look, Tansy, is this relevant? June died, and now Gemma's got some hang-up about it. Is it relevant how June died?'

'Of course it is! If she'd been—say—murdered, it would affect Gemma. If she'd suffered a long, lingering illness, it would also have some effect. However she died, Gemma would——'

'But Gemma doesn't know how. We never told her. We just said June had gone to hospital, but she didn't get better.'

'She accepted that?' asked Tansy.

'She seemed to.'

'So why did June go to hospital, Nicholas?'

'All right, since you insist. June committed suicide.'

Tansy stared at him, horrified. Suicide!

'Because she thought she had cancer?'

'No! She never thought she had cancer. A—nervous disease. It isn't important. But it made her anxious and irritable and clumsy.'

'And depressed. She must have been terribly depressed.'

'It wasn't apparent. Look, Tansy, I don't have much time——' Nicholas glanced at his watch '—and we seem to be getting off the subject. Gemma doesn't know how or why June died, so I think we can safely put it out of our minds. Could her disturbance simply be an expression of grief?'

'It could,' Tansy agreed.

'So we have to work her through it, get her to express her fears.'

'Yes. But, Nicholas, I'm the psychiatrist, let me do it my way. All right?'

He stood up, a strange expression in his eyes. 'Naturally. Anything more I need to know?'

'Not that I can think of.'

'Then I'll be going.' But, instead of going towards the door, he moved round to her side of the desk. Tansy struggled to her feet. She felt at a disadvantage with him towering over her. Yet standing put her into a more embarrassing situation because her face was now only inches from his.

'I would have liked to stay longer,' he began, his sharp eyes seeming to search her face. Tansy held her breath. Just a step forward. . . Then he turned and went across to the door.

'When do you want to see her again?' he asked.

'I haven't really decided.' She flipped the pages of her appointment book, not seeing anything. 'Perhaps—tomorrow——'

'Impossible. Neither of us could collect her. And later there's Biff Weston's engagement party.'

'Oh, yes!' Tansy had had an invitation, but, as usual, had decided not to go.

'You're going?' queried Nicholas.

'Don't sound surprised! I do go to parties.'

'I'll see you there, then. Perhaps you can give me a date then.'

He closed the door behind him. A date? He wanted a date? Yes—he had said he wasn't going to give up. Then Tansy smiled to herself. He hadn't meant a date with her at all! He'd been talking about Gemma.

She started to clear away the modelling clay and paints, and found herself mentally revising her wardrobe, wondering what she should wear for Barry Weston's party. Barry—nicknamed Biff because of some past rugby misdeameanour, apparently—was junior registrar on Mr Wakefield's surgical team, and his fiancée was a staff nurse on Casualty, Angela Something-or-other. Tansy didn't see much of the Casualty staff, but she recalled Angela as being auburn-haired and a bit chubby, with a definite likeness to a certain member of the Royal Family.

She wondered about her kingfisher-blue dress. It had always suited her, even though it was a few years old. She always felt comfortable in it, with its loose bloused top and crinkle-pleated skirt. Yes, the kingfisher blue. And her navy sandals. And the bright blue and silver necklace Rod had bought her, only a few weeks before. . . She bit her lip, wishing everything didn't still remind her, and picked up the screwed-up painting Gemma had done.

Lost in thought, she flattened it out and spread it on a table. The sleeping figure, lying on what seemed to be a couch, now revealed itself to be staring blankly out of the picture at her with wide, pale eyes. The hair seemed to be a yellowish-brown colour, and the face definitely jaundiced. Was this intentional, or could it be that Gemma couldn't make a better skin tone? She was only six, after all. Just six. And she'd been sick on her birthday. Hadn't Gemma said it had been only last week? Yes, when she herself was in the Lake District, trying to come to terms with a swarm of traumatic memories.

The black figures in the painting seemed to resemble witches, with their pointed hats and white faces. Even the one in yellow had a black hat—or was it hair? This one didn't have its hands over its face, but was grinning quite obscenely, with lots of white teeth. Or perhaps Gemma found difficulty in painting smiling mouths. Teeth were difficult, Tansy recalled from her schooldays. She'd never got the hang of painting faces. Or anything, for that matter.

There was something else in the painting she hadn't noticed before, on the ground, near the supine figure in red, among the pool of snowflakes. Looked a bit like writing. Tansy held the painting to the light. Yes. The letters were small and shaky. M-U-W- no, another M- a small g? No. Tansy stared in horror. M-U-M-Y. Mummy.

So this was June as Gemma remembered her. The poor, poor child! No wonder she was disturbed. Surely they hadn't allowed her to see June after she'd died? The horror of it made her shudder. She'd have to mention it to Nicholas. She began to fold up the painting. Why hadn't she shown it to him? True, he had been in a hurry. Still——

Then she noticed more writing, near the figure in yellow, the grinning figure. Male? Female? Impossible to tell. But the letters, although uneven and childish, were quite clear to decipher. And Tansy recalled how upset Gemma had been when she had finished the painting, almost as though her fears had surfaced, and she couldn't face them.

'She killed her! She's dead. And she killed her!'

The face of the yellow figure was spoiled now, by an overlay of red lines, but the word was clear. G-E-M-M-A.

By the time Friday morning arrived, Tansy had almost put the disturbing painting out of her mind. It had not been easy, when most of her waking thoughts centred on the evening's party, and seeing Nicholas again. Thinking of Nicholas reminded her of Gemma, and then the painting. She wished she had shown it to him. But he might not interpret the picture in the same way. Lots of children had vivid and gory imaginations. He might argue that she was getting it out of her system by painting it, even if it wasn't true.

Hey, who's the psychiatrist? she argued. But she determinedly put it out of her mind, and concentrated on looking forward to the party.

She looked at herself, in the kingfisher dress and the high-heeled navy sandals. Was it a bit old-fashioned? What were people wearing these days? Lurex and black satin trousers? She didn't possess such items. And even the navy sandals were past their best. Still, she didn't intend to do any violent disco dancing. She took a deep breath. It was ages since she'd been to a party. Was it still noisy disco dancing, or had something else superseded it?

She twisted about in front of the mirror. What about the plum velvet? No, too hot for a party. So there was only the black cocktail dress her mother had chosen, and that was even older than this! She realised her wardrobe was sadly lacking. Oh, well, the blue always suited her. And there was always the possibility that she wouldn't get to dance with Nicholas. Surely he wouldn't be going alone? The staff nurse she'd once seen him with? Tansy felt a violent, irrational reaction at the thought, and almost pulled off the blue frock.

No, I shan't go. There's no point. I shall just stand and watch people, and get under their feet.

Then she recalled his expression when she'd told him she was going. Delighted? Or just surprised? No, he had looked pleased. So blow them all, she'd go. And what if he did take someone? She chuckled. Perhaps he'd take the housekeeper!

She turned back to the mirror and carefully applied lilac and turquoise eye-shadow, and clover-pink lipstick. Her eyes seemed to be an even darker shade of violet than usual tonight.

She fingered the blue and silver necklace Rod had given her seven years before. The aquamarines and clear spinels caught the light as she moved. Was it really so long? Yet the memory was as clear as ever. It would be seven years in August, the day he'd gone. August the third. She had watched him leave in his red sports car, heading for Reading and his new post. He'd had big plans, Rod had. Ambitious plans to become a famous neuro-surgeon. He could have done it.

He had worn an emerald-green shirt that day, which, against the scarlet of the car, looked almost Christmassy. He had never seen another Christmas. And Tansy's

Christmas had been very different from the one she had planned. But she had waved to him happily from her mother's house, calling to him to remember to phone that evening.

Instead of the phone call, it had been two police officers. They had found her name and address in his pocket. Almost worse than all that was the news that he hadn't been going to Reading at all. And he hadn't been alone.

Tansy rose quickly from the stool, pushing her memories behind her. If she didn't hurry she'd be late. Although it didn't really matter at these parties, if they were anything like the ones she used to attend. Guests came and went as they liked. Be honest, she told herself. You want to be early in case Nicholas is early. Her colour deepened and she went to get her coat.

She could hear the music from the street when she arrived, and hoped Biff had understanding neighbours! He was an extremely likeable fellow, easygoing and generous. It would have been difficult to dislike him. And very likely that most of his neighbours had been invited.

That idea was strengthened when Tansy hung up her coat in the second-floor hall, and entered the room, because most of the guests already there were complete strangers to her. It all went quiet as she stepped through the door, and she had an eerie feeling that she hadn't been expected. Or she'd got a smut on her face!

But Biff came hurrying towards her, smiling widely, and she was aware that conversation had started again. She must have imagined it. Why should she effect such a sudden silence?

'So glad you could come, Tansy!' He took her hand, and his blue eyes laughed. 'You know Angie, don't you?'

A plump, auburn-haired girl had appeared at his side, and a name flew unbidden into Tansy's mind. Christina Swallow. But this was Angela Something-or-other, a staff nurse in Casualty. Why should she think of Christina Swallow now? She'd never even seen the girl. And it had been years since she'd thought about her. She smiled at Angela, and congratulated them, and accepted a glass of white wine.

She must have thought of Rod, she decided. Must have caught a glimpse of black curly hair. Or perhaps an emerald-green shirt. Every time she saw a red sports car, or an emerald-green shirt. . . She sipped her drink, looking around her for a familiar face. But they were mostly just people she'd seen from a distance, in the corridors, in the laboratories. They didn't know her, and made no effort to come and talk to her. She felt like going home again.

The seats around the sides of the room were occupied; other guests were standing and talking. No one was dancing yet, although the music was lively and rhythmic. No sign of Nicholas. And the room was filling rapidly. She made her way to the makeshift bar to return her glass, and find a quiet corner where she could watch arrivals undisturbed. A hand took her arm.

'Hello, Tansy. Didn't expect to see you here.' She turned quickly. Daniel Rice—in a bright green silk shirt. Emerald-green. She tore her eyes away from it and smiled at him.

'That's a very striking shirt, Dr Rice,' she observed.

'The name's Daniel, off duty. Do you like it? I thought it was a bit bright, but I was told it was the fashion. I'm a bit out of touch with things like fashion—don't go to enough of these do's. I get too wrapped up in my work. It's a bad mistake to make, Tansy. There's more to life than the hospital.'

'I'm sure you're quite right—Daniel.' Still no sign of Nicholas.

'So I've decided to come out of my shell now and again. Which is what you seem to have done, Tansy.'

'Oh, I don't have a shell,' she assured him.

He smiled, sipped his drink, and narrowed his icy

blue eyes. 'No, I do believe you're soft centre through and through.'

'Not quite as soft as that. More like a—piece of nougat.'

'I see. Pliable, with little bits of hardness here and there? What a fascinating character! Do you think we could use the same analogy for all these people here, Tansy? Now Biff—he's got to be a piece of fudge. And Angela—perhaps a chewy toffee? Oh, and that girl over there, in the pink, obviously marshmallow. I wonder what I am?'

'Peanut brittle?'

He gave a wry smile. 'Is it really so obvious? I do try to hide the sweetness. But nougat, that's interesting. I wonder where all the little hard bits have come from?'

His voice was soft and almost hypnotic. Tansy could understand why he was such a good psychiatrist. She laughed, a little too loudly.

'Are you trying to analyse me, Dan?'

'I'm sure it would be a fascinating project. You're a bit of an enigma, you know. Oh, they're starting to dance—a nice smoochy one. Coming?'

Reluctantly, Tansy left the safety of her corner and went on to the floor with Dan. One dance. She'd have one dance with him. It wouldn't last all night.

He was an excellent dancer, despite his lack of practice, and she found it easy to follow his steps. She'd never liked ballroom dancing much. She'd always felt everyone was looking at her. Dan was talking quietly in her ear, about another party he'd been to, a long time ago, when he'd been newly qualified, and she tried to concentrate on what he was saying. But her gaze was constantly drawn towards the doorway. More people were arriving. How on earth was Biff going to get them all in?

She stiffened. A familiar chestnut head was visible above the others. Her heart began to race. She hoped Dan didn't misinterpret her sudden tenseness. If only the music would end! He was there—in a deep gold shirt. He was talking and laughing, looking down at someone. Tansy could just see the top of a blonde head.

Dan changed direction, and Tansy lost sight of Nicholas. When she got a view of the doorway again, he had moved. Then the dance ended, and Tansy could see Dan was fully expecting her to dance the next one with him. And the next one. And she visualised herself never getting a chance to talk to Nicholas, just glimpses of him as she was whirled around the floor. There was plenty of female company here tonight for him to bestow his favours on. She hadn't yet seen the staff nurse he'd once taken out, but she had seen Sister Rudge, who was very attractive. And single.

She shrugged her shoulders. Why should it concern her that the sister of Male Surgical was attractive and single? She had no intention of getting deeply involved again. And hadn't she told Nicholas that? All she wanted right now was to enjoy her little infatuation while it lasted, make the most of it before it brought her pain. As it surely would. At least it proved she was still alive, still capable of affection.

The music was starting again, and Dan took her arm.

'Excuse me, Dan. I must go to the cloakroom,' Tansy said hurriedly.

He didn't say anything, just turned away and crossed to the bar—in reality, a long sideboard, behind which presided a fat young man in a bow tie.

As she threaded her way between the dancers, Tansy hoped Nicholas wouldn't catch sight of her. He would stop her to talk, and Dan Rice would know her departure had just been an excuse. And she didn't want to hurt him. She liked him, and she didn't want to make things awkward during their working hours.

It was all so difficult, being a woman doctor, she told herself as she slipped through the door. There wouldn't have been any of these problems if she'd been a man.

She stood for a few moments in the empty bathroom, and, after dabbing some powder on her nose—in case anyone came in and saw her just standing there—she judged she had been away long enough. As she returned, a couple were leaving early, making their apologies to Biff and Angela at the door. Tansy squeezed inside, and someone immediately put a hand on her shoulder. And she knew who it was. She turned to face him, her skin tingling at the contact.

'Nicholas—you made it!'

'Of course. Didn't I promise I'd see you here? You're looking quite delectable. Good enough to eat.'

'I've already been compared with a piece of nougat,' she said, blushing.

'Spare me the details! Didn't I see you dancing with your venerable superior, Daniel Rice?'

'I'm not sure he'd approve of being called venerable,' she smiled.

'Well, of course, I meant it in the true sense of the word—venerated, respected. But why are we talking about him? There are other topics more interesting. Gosh, it's noisy in here! Impossible to talk about anything. Do you really want to dance, Tansy?'

She forced herself to answer nonchalantly. 'I'm not a very good dancer.'

'Then let's go out here and talk.' Taking her hand, Nicholas led her between the prancing couples—it was modern disco dancing now—and she was acutely aware of the pressure of his fingers. All right, she told herself, infatuation it might be, but she still had to stay in control. No letting things get out of hand.

They were out on the balcony now, and Nicholas turned and quite deliberately closed the door behind them. Tansy shivered. She made a token protest.

'Nicholas, is this wise?'

'What do you mean? Is what wise?'

'You know what I mean—bringing me out here. People will talk.'

'People will always talk. But haven't we come out here precisely for that? Surely you didn't think I'd brought you out here with more intimate intentions on my mind?'

'Well, of course I didn't——' she rushed to defend herself.

'Then why are you breathing like that?' He moved closer. 'And I can see a little pulse—just there——' and he touched her neck '—and it's far too fast for normal. I do believe you did think that. And what's so terrible about it? What do you expect me to do?'

His voice was low and caressing. His eyes seemed to glitter in the twilight.

'Nicholas—don't you remember——?' But he had taken her in his arms, and she could feel his heart beating, almost as fast as her own. She struggled feebly. She couldn't let him think——

'Of course I remember. You want a platonic relationship. But don't you remember what I said? I was making no promises to agree to that.'

'That's not gentlemanly!'

'Do you really want a gentleman, Tansy? How can you say such things, under that perfectly good moon, and those sentimental stars? You don't really mean it, do you? Come on, hand on heart and swear.'

Tansy couldn't help smiling, even though she felt she was losing control.

'Leave my heart out of it,' she said shakily.

'Now that's a thing I can't do.' Then she was in his arms, his lips caressed hers, softly at first, then with more passion, as his hands stroked her body, and it was just as she had imagined, and she knew she was going to lose control; her head felt it was bursting, those sentimental stars were behind her eyes now, and her skin was on fire.

Then his mouth slowly relinquished hers. Her knees felt weak, and she clung to him, trembling. Even Rod had never made her feel like this. Yet she had loved Rod, and this had to be mere infatuation. Had to be. She didn't believe she could love twice.

'That wasn't fair!' she protested weakly. 'You took advantage of me.'

Nicholas studied her seriously. 'I only did what you wanted.'

'But you promised——'

'I didn't promise anything, if you recall. I don't make promises lightly.' His voice was shaking slightly as he said softly, 'I could never make those sort of promises with someone like you.'

'I wanted a professional relationship.'

'We already have one. I send my patients to you because I believe you're the best registrar in child psychiatry we've had for a long time. And because—because it's an excuse to get to know you better.'

'Oh, you're insufferable!' Tansy pulled herself away from him and crossed to the balcony rail, where she looked out at the lights of the town. She was full of doubt. Against her better judgement she wanted his kisses, his caresses. But she couldn't ignore the little voice that warned her, reminded her of what had happened last time she had given in to her desires, and the agony it had brought. It couldn't happen again. She wouldn't let it happen again.

So she kept her voice steady as she said, 'You led me to believe you brought me out here to talk. About Gemma?'

'About us.'

'Then I think we've done it all.' She turned back to face him.

'We haven't even started.'

'Didn't you understand what I told you on Wednesday? There isn't any point in it. Can't you let things stay as they are?'

'But surely you must see, Tansy, that things have moved on somewhat since Wednesday? As I see it, it's going to be virtually impossible to leave things as they are. What are you afraid of, Tansy? Relationships? Or just relationships with men?'

'It's none of your business—or anyone else's! Just leave me alone, and keep out of my life!'

She turned suddenly, and her foot caught on the rail

of the balcony. She wrenched it free, cursing under her breath, and the strap of her sandal tore away.

'Damn!' she muttered, pulling the sandal from her foot. At the same moment she began to lose her balance, and it was Nicholas's strong arm that reached out and held her against him for support. It was then the balcony door burst open, and a voice said, in some surprise, 'So you're here, Nicholas! I've been looking for you everywhere!'

Tansy's head jerked up. There stood quite the most attractive girl she had ever seen, platinum hair in Grecian style, slim-fitting scarlet dress, and long, long legs. In the same instant she realised it was the girl who had arrived with him. And she felt a cold lump settle in her stomach.

CHAPTER SIX

'NICHOLAS, what on earth are you doing out here? You know you promised me a tango. I had to do it with that awful little man from X-Ray. And you promised!'

Tansy suddenly found her voice. 'Shame on you, Nicholas,' she said teasingly. 'Did you really promise?'

She was satisfied to see him looking distinctly uncomfortable. The girl seemed to notice Tansy for the first time, and she frowned.

'Yes, he did promise,' she said grumpily. Tansy looked at her, seeing not a girl, but a woman of at least thirty. Those little lines around the mouth and the eyes, lines of—suffering?

'Then you must keep your promise, Nicholas,' she said, smiling at him.

'Don't I get a chance to join in this conversation, or is it girls only?' said Nicholas wryly.

'Come on, Nicholas,' pleaded the blonde girl. She wasn't the staff nurse, thought Tansy. 'First you were closeted with that bone fellow for ages, and now I find you out here, doing I don't know what.' Her gaze took in Tansy's blue dress and the broken sandal. And Nicholas's arm still supporting her. Tansy moved quickly away, resting her stockinged foot on the ground.

'As a matter of fact, Beth, we were discussing Gemma,' he said.

Beth! Tansy felt as though she'd been hit by a sledgehammer. So this was Beth, plump, homely, middle-aged Beth, in the print pinafore, and flour-covered arms. This was Beth! Didn't the neighbours talk?

'A likely story,' said Beth, laughing and taking his arm. 'Come on, they're going to play some Scottish reels soon.'

'I don't think you understand, Beth. We were talking about Gemma.' Tansy refused to correct the lie. 'This is Tansy Blair, the psychiatrist.'

Beth's eyes widened. 'Tansy Blair? Golly, I never expected her to look like you!'

Tansy smiled and held out her hand. 'The feeling's mutual.' She found she was beginning to like the girl, despite still reacting to the shock. Beth shook her hand firmly.

'Gemma—the poor kid! Can you help her?'

'I'm pretty sure I can. I'll do my best. And may I compliment you on the delicious meal you prepared for us?'

Beth shrugged her shoulders. 'It was nothing. I used to be a cordon bleu cook, a long time ago.' She turned back to Nicholas. 'Are we going to dance or not?'

'Beth, you know I'm not a good dancer. And——' he glanced at Tansy, and caught sight of the broken sandal in her hand '—besides, Tansy has broken her strap. You can't expect me to just leave her here, standing on one foot like a stork!'

Tansy resisted a giggle. Beth reached out and took the sandal, and examined it critically in the light from the door.

'Just needs a few stitches,' she pronounced. 'How on earth did you break it?'

Tansy flushed. 'Oh, I turned my ankle suddenly. I should have checked them before I came out—they're pretty ancient.'

'They look it. Sorry, didn't mean to be rude.'

'Beth's a bit outspoken at times,' Nicholas explained.

'Come on,' ordered Beth. 'I've got needle and thread in my bag, I'll mend it for you. Can you hop?'

'Like a frog,' murmured Tansy, and was mollified by a low laugh from Nicholas.

And strangely enough, it was the Frog Song they were playing as they made their way between the crowds, perhaps slightly less now, and into the bathroom. The toilet, fortunately, was separate, so they didn't have to vacate it every few moments. Tansy sat on the edge of the bath, while Beth searched in her black velvet bag, and soon produced a very practical but small étui. She opened it, sat on the cork-topped stool, and bit off some black thread.

'When did you last wear these strappy sandals?' she asked, threading a needle.

'Oh, some time ago—I've had them ages. But I don't go to many parties, so I didn't think it worthwhile to splash out on new ones.'

'Or even a new frock,' remarked Beth, starting to sew deftly.

Tansy flushed. 'I expect it's a bit dated,' she admitted. 'But I've always liked the colour.'

'The colour suits you, I suppose,' Beth agreed. 'But it's not today's colour. Certainly not today's style.'

Tansy shrugged. 'It seems one can get away with anything these days—trousers, caftans, smocks. I didn't think anyone would notice this dress.'

'I don't suppose they did, more's the pity. Because they should have noticed you, with your looks.'

Tansy forbore from reminding Beth that Nicholas had found her very attractive tonight. Instead she said, 'They noticed you. Red suits you. I have to admit, I didn't expect you to look as you do.'

Beth laughed. 'And I expected you to be grey-haired with steel-rimmed spectacles!' She sewed busily. 'But, you know, you could make more of yourself. More make-up, colours that complement your hair, and your eyes——' She glanced up as she spoke, looking straight at Tansy. 'Gosh, I didn't notice that before. Your eyes—almost violet, aren't they? So very similar. Such a lovely colour.' She stared quizzically at her for a moment, before returning to her task. Tansy was beginning to feel uncomfortable. What had Beth meant?

'Yes,' Beth continued blithely, 'try some different colours. A strong jewel blue, a sea-green. And your hair—try a different style. You look about sixteen. I'm surprised the patients don't wonder if you're qualified.'

'My patients are children,' said Tansy stiffly. 'And I really don't need any more clothes.'

'Won't you be going to parties with Nicholas?'

Tansy was taken aback. 'With Nicholas? Why should I? Doesn't he usually take you?'

'Only now and again—I've got my own circle of friends. I got the impression you two were getting on quite well together.'

'It's just a working relationship,' said Tansy. 'Oh, you've finished it.'

'Said it wouldn't take long.' Beth bit off the thread, but didn't hand the sandal back. She looked speculatively at Tansy.

'Tansy's an unusual name,' she said musingly.

'A flower name.'

'That's right, Gemma told us. A big yellow daisy.'

'More like a dandelion, really,' laughed Tansy, gratified that Gemma should have been so impressed by her visit.

'Wild flowers are beautiful,' said Beth unexpectedly.

'Of course. I'm very fond of wild flowers. Used to collect them at school—special project we had, collect as many as you could, some girls got as many as two hundred——' Tansy tailed off, aware that she was rambling. Beth was smiling, but eyeing her curiously. She still held the navy sandal, almost as if it were a hostage, thought Tansy.

'Do you like Nicholas?' she asked suddenly.

'He's an excellent doctor.'

'That wasn't what I asked. Well, never mind. I was thinking about your name. Tansy. I've heard it before.'

'Really?' Tansy was only too keen to change the topic of conversation. Later, she wished she hadn't.

'In the States—America.'

'I'm surprised it's surfaced there,' said Tansy brightly. 'I thought most of their names were our thirties and forties names. You know—Susan, Carol, Doris, Barbara——' Her mother's letter. Richard and Babs. Little girl of six. Francine.

'Well, yes, you're right, I suppose,' Beth agreed. 'But I didn't meet a person named Tansy.'

'Not a dog!'

Beth laughed politely. 'No, I met a couple when I visited the Smoky Mountains. Ever heard of the Smoky Mountains?'

'No, never.' A cold finger of dread was tracing along Tansy's spine. America. But it was such a huge country. . .

'I was modelling over there—did Nicholas tell you?' Beth continued. 'We were doing magazine shots in the National Park—Fontana Lake. You must visit there, Tansy, the scenery is out of this world.'

'I have no ambitions to work in America.'

'No? Well, about this couple I met. Middle-aged, very friendly. She was English, you see, and he was American —her second marriage. Ted, his name was. A funny little man.'

'Funny' wasn't how Tansy would have described him, knowing immediately what had happened. And she marvelled how, out of the millions and millions of people in America, Beth had had to meet her mother. Unless— another Ted? Not her mother? Yet she instinctively knew it was. She smiled.

'How nice for you,' she murmured. 'Another Englishwoman.'

'Oh, there are lots over there. No, the coincidence was, she has a daughter named Tansy.'

'So my name's not as original as I thought.'

'A doctor in England,' Beth added.

'That is amazing. Er—what was her name, this Englishwoman?'

'Connie. Connie Baxter.' Tansy kept a fixed, unruffled smile on her face. Beth went on happily. 'She told me such a lot about herself, how she'd been a widow for years, then had met Ted on a package tour of Greece, and it was love at first sight.'

Yes, thought Tansy, I've heard all that too.

'Of course,' said Beth, 'she never got round to telling

me her name before she married Ted, so I've no idea what her daughter's other name is.'

Tansy couldn't help feeling that was a lie, and Beth knew quite well who she was. But she had to go along with the pretence, couldn't admit now that her mother was Connie Baxter.

'It isn't really relevant,' she said, through dry lips. 'Because my mother's name is Jean. And she didn't go to——' Oh, hell, how had she got into this? This was what lying did for you. It just got worse and worse as you went on. Beth was waiting for her to finish.

'To that part of America—Carolina. She went to—California. Los Angeles.'

'California! I was there too.'

Tansy felt trapped, in a spider's web.

'Lovely part of the country, the West Coast.' She stood up, feeling awkward, as one leg was three inches shorter than the other. She sat again.

'Sure is. But, Tansy, you said you'd never heard of the Smoky Mountains. So how did you know they were in Carolina?'

Tansy just wanted to run away and hide. This was ten times worse than any job interview! But she knew she had to bluff it out. Or confess. And then Nicholas would get to know, about Rod, about everything. It didn't bear thinking about.

'What a lucky guess!' she shrugged. 'I suppose I must have read about them somewhere, subconsciously remembered it. Amazing thing, the memory. Fancy them being in Carolina!'

But Beth seemed to have lost interest. She was folding up her little sewing kit. The sandal lay on the floor, and Tansy grabbed it and put it on.

'You've made a good job of the strap,' she said lightly.

Beth stood up. 'May I ask you something, Tansy?'

'Fire away.' Couldn't be worse than before.

'Are you going to make a career of medicine?'

'Of course I am,' said Tansy. 'It's taken me nine years to reach my position so far.'

'And where does marriage fit into your plans? And children?'

'At the moment, nowhere. Nor in the foreseeable future. As for children, I have all the children I need in my job.'

Beth nodded. 'Good. Now I'm going to be frank. I'd be obliged if you don't lead Nicholas into believing he has a chance with you.'

'You're too late,' said Tansy. 'I've already told him.'

'That's very wise of you, Tansy. Nicholas's happiness means a lot to me. I don't intend to see him get hurt.'

'I'm sure you're very sincere in your intentions,' said Tansy. 'But, as his housekeeper, don't you think you're getting a bit above yourself?'

Beth laughed. 'You thought I was just his house-keeper? Well, yes, I suppose I am in a way. But I'd rather think of myself as being a bit more than that. We were once engaged.'

'Why didn't you marry?'

Beth looked away. 'It's personal—I changed my mind. I went to the States. And while I was away, he married June.'

'On the rebound, you mean? Then he must have been very hurt.'

'I don't know. I felt hurt. I hated June for a while, even more when Gemma arrived. But then, later—well, I could see how it had happened.'

Tansy frowned. 'I've never met anyone like you, Beth. Didn't you feel any revenge in your heart? Or didn't you love him any more? Was that why you changed your mind?'

Beth seemed to slump against the washbasin. 'That wasn't why I went away. It was because I loved him that I went away. I can't explain in a few words, but you wouldn't be interested.'

'So how could you come back here, while June was still alive, and look after her, and the house? Did you know she was going to die?' Tansy persisted.

'How could I? She killed herself. Did you perhaps think I killed her?'

'Of course not!' protested Tansy.

'It was Valium—an overdose.'

'But to be in the same house as her, knowing he loved her and not you——'

'He didn't love June,' said Beth. 'Not after I came back. And not for the reason you're thinking. You see, I had to come back. There were certain things I had to tell him about June.'

'I'm surprised she let you stay in the house,' said Tansy drily.

'She wanted me there. She wrote to me, asking me to come back, and she knew all the time that I'd tell him what she should have told him before she married him. She accepted it.'

'She wrote to you? Weren't you the last person——?'

'She was desperate,' Beth explained. 'I was the only one who could help her. I see from your puzzlement, Tansy, that Nicholas hasn't told you about us. June and I were sisters.'

CHAPTER SEVEN

FOR a moment Tansy couldn't speak. Beth and June—sisters? She swallowed.

'But June was—well, you weren't a bit alike! I saw June, in a photograph, and she was——'

'Quite plain? Well, I'm no raving beauty myself, but June, unfortunately, took after our father—in more ways than one, I expect.' Beth spoke harshly.

'What do you mean?' asked Tansy.

'Nothing of importance. It's just that Father died quite young, and June thought she was going——'

'But she did die young—by her own hand.'

'She was a hypochondriac. Always had been,' shrugged Beth.

'Did no one reassure her that she wasn't seriously ill?'

'Have you ever tried reassuring a hypochrondriac? Of course they did. But I don't want to talk about June, it depresses me. Let's go back to the others.'

By the time they reached the party again, Beth had quickly changed the subject to food. Listening to her, Tansy was surprised when a green shirt bore down on them.

'Tansy! Where have you been hiding yourself? I thought you'd gone home.' But his eyes were on Beth.

'I broke my sandal,' Tansy explained. 'Beth has very kindly mended it for me. Oh, have you met Beth, Dr—Daniel?'

'Many times. But once more will be a bonus. Red suits you, Miss Gadsby. Would you care to dance? I believe it's a tango.'

'A tango!'

Relieved that Beth would get her dance at last, Tansy couldn't hep wondering where Nicholas was. At the same time, she couldn't forget what Beth had said about

Connie. Her mother had never been known for her discretion, but what about Beth? Had she told Nicholas everything? Dared she face him again?

She made her way to the makeshift bar and ordered an orange juice. She stood in the corner, sipping it, blankly watching the wildly gyrating dancers. She saw Dan and Beth, and they seemed to be enjoying themselves. Beth was a better dancer than herself. Beth seemed to be better than herself at most things, she reflected. And she found herself wondering why she had rushed off to America, when it was obvious she was still in love with Nicholas. So why didn't she marry him now? June was dead, there was no one standing in her way.

And I'm not, Beth Gadsby, she reminded herself. Gadsby: that name seemed to ring a bell. Gadsby Gadgets? Could it be? Well, that would explain a lot of things. Nicholas's luxurious house, for a start. And Beth's own expensive tastes. And she didn't have a job, did she? No need for one.

Tansy tried to remember all she could about the self-made millionaire, George Gadsby. He had started by inventing the simplest of potato-peelers, and then gone on to even more simple but time-saving gadgets that no one else had, surprisingly, ever thought of before. Yes, he had died young. In his early forties? Heart attack? thought Tansy. No—it was coming back to her, it had been in all the papers, but a long time ago, when she'd been at school. A hospital on the south coast—no, not a hospital, a nursing home, a—a psychiatric nursing home! Was that what Beth had meant? Were they George Gadsby's daughters? So June had been afraid of developing a mental illness. Yes, it fitted. Poor June. And could Beth be worried for the same reason? It seemed unlikely; she seemed unnaturally sane, if there was such a thing. Yet she hadn't wanted to talk about it. But that wasn't surprising. Mental illness was still a stigma to lots of people, although the situation was improving.

Gemma. Oh, God—Gemma! Was that why they had

called her in? Could it be that Nicholas and Beth suspected the child's disturbance was a symptom of something more than grief? Was that why he had been so reluctant to tell her how June had died? He thought Gemma had inherited the weakness? It was no good, she'd have to tackle him about it. It was time he told her the whole truth.

And, as she made this decision, Tansy caught sight of his gold shirt and wavy chestnut hair, crossing the floor towards her. She looked at his face and knew it was all too late. At that instant she knew it wasn't infatuation at all. She was in love with him.

He joined her at the bar. 'What are you having?' he asked. She refused another drink, and he ordered a non-alcoholic grape juice.

'I'm glad to see you got on with Beth,' Nicholas remarked.

'Yes—I like her. Nicholas, you didn't tell me she was June's sister.'

He raised his eyebrows. 'Didn't I? Well, it isn't really important, is it?'

'You were engaged to her.'

'She broke it off. Tansy, all this makes no difference to us, does it?'

'Of course it doesn't. How can it? We just have a perfectly amicable relationship.' She hoped he didn't sense the churning emotions inside her.

'I see your sandal is adequately repaired,' he remarked, glancing at her foot. 'You have very nice ankles, Tansy.'

She ignored that remark. 'Yes, Beth is very good with her hands. As you told me before.'

'Do I detect a glimmer of jealousy there?' he queried, his eyes twinkling.

'I detect an oversized ego,' Tansy retorted. 'Why should I be jealous of Beth? Why should I be jealous of anyone? I have a satisfying career, I meet lots of interesting people——'

'Including me,' he put in.

'—I'm reasonably well paid, I have foreign holidays whenever I want——'

'Hey, hey, why are you so much on the defensive?' He reached out and held her arms, his expression puzzled.

'I'm not on the defensive. I'm just explaining——'

'But you missed something out. You didn't list a satisfying social life. Or a satisfying relationship. Don't they matter to you, Tansy?'

'My social life is fine, Nicholas,' she said touchily. 'And so are my relationships.' She moved smartly out of his grasp. 'And I'd be obliged if you'd stop prying into my private life!'

She hurried across the room, between the dancers, part of her hoping he'd call her back. But he didn't, and, still smarting, she collected her coat and ran down the stairs. It was her own fault. She'd done what she'd vowed never to do again: she'd fallen in love, and it was leading to heartbreak. Perhaps it wasn't too late, after all. Perhaps she could still stop it, and keep her heart in one piece.

She ran along the pavement towards her car.

The next day was Saturday, and Tansy made up her mind to clear it of anything to do with the hospital. She'd wander round the shops, get some groceries in, perhaps visit the library. Then she'd put her feet up, read a good book or watch television. It sounded enjoyable. So why did she feel so restless?

She'd write letters on Sunday. She owed her friend Mary one, at the Royal Hampshire. Janice in Scotland— she was an old school friend she hadn't seen for years. Might be a good idea to invite her down for a few days in the summer. Oh, and she'd better reply to her mother's letter, while she was about it.

And that, of course, reminded her of Beth, and ruined her resolution. And she couldn't stop convincing herself that Connie had told Beth all about Southampton, and Rod, and everything else, and that Beth had told Nicholas. The whole thing seemed to have grown into a gigantic nightmare that she couldn't throw off. It seemed so enormous, her whole life must depend on Beth's accepting her lies. She hated lying, but it seemed the only thing to do, to stop her world all turning topsy-turvy.

She turned on the radio to drown her thoughts. Simon and Garfunkel were singing 'Bridge Over Troubled Water'.

'Oh, yes,' she said to the orange juice, 'that's me, all right. Troubled water!'

It was a sunny April day, between the showers, so Tansy slipped on a showerproof jacket over blue shirt and jeans, and went down to the shops. She walked, because parking could be a problem.

It was after ten o'clock, and the streets were thronged with shoppers. She spent a leisurely half-hour in the supermarket, filling her basket with salad, eggs, bread and milk. At the last moment she added a large bar of milk chocolate. It wasn't often that she ate sweets. She had to be in the mood. Eating for comfort?

She emerged into a heavy shower, and retreated into a tea-shop for shelter. The smell of coffee and cakes kindled her taste-buds. The shower seemed likely to last some time, so she decided to have a drink.

She found a seat by the window, and quite enjoyed watching the scurrying people outside, as she languished over her coffee. Such bright colours, raincoats and umbrellas and plastic carrier bags.

A child in a vivid red hooded raincoat came skipping past as she watched, the hood pulled over her dark hair. For a moment Tansy thought it was Gemma. The child came running back, her face tilted as someone called to her. It was Gemma! Tansy's heart seemed to skip a beat. But she didn't want to see her! She'd be with Beth, or Nicholas, and that would uncover all her raw emotions again.

Gemma turned and looked straight through the window of the shop, her face expectant, her finger pointing at the variety of cakes displayed. Tansy turned away, pretending to look for something in her bag. From the corner of her eye, she could see the red raincoat had been joined by a pale one, a beige one. Not Beth's colour. . .

She kept her head averted, and when she finally dared to look round they had gone. She sighed with relief, and drank some more coffee. Her heart was racing. She settled back in her seat and gazed out again at the shoppers. She smiled to herself as a very small boy in a blue anorak was hauled along the pavement by a huge Irish wolfhound, much bigger than himself.

'Hello, Dr Tansy!'

Tansy looked round quickly.

'Why, Gemma! Fancy seeing you here. Are you buying cakes for tea?'

'Not for tea.' Gemma plumped herself down opposite Tansy and pulled back her hood. Drops of rain clung to the black curls on her forehead. She grinned at Tansy.

'Oh, you're stopping for coffee? Tea?' At the shop counter, Nicholas was paying for purchases.

'We weren't going to, but I saw you through the window,' Gemma explained. 'Didn't you see me? I waved.'

'No. No, I didn't,' said Tansy.

'So I told Daddy, and he said why didn't we go and join her? And here we are.'

Tansy couldn't stop the warm feeling that spread through her. It had been Nicholas's suggestion. Oh, why had he done it? Couldn't he see he was making it more painful for her?

'Well, it's very nice, Gemma,' she said, finishing her coffee hastily. 'But I was just about to go——'

'You can't do that,' came Nicholas's voice behind her. 'Not now we've arrived.' His voice sent a little shiver through her. She smiled at him as he laid a tray on the table and transferred the contents. Gemma reached out for a pink milkshake and an iced bun.

'More coffee, Tansy?' asked Nicholas, removing the tray.

'No, thank you. I've been here too long. I must go——' But he was already slipping into the seat beside her, barring her way out. She moved away to give him more room. His proximity was disturbing.

He turned and smiled artlessly at her, and bit into a Danish pastry. She was hemmed in, with Gemma on one side, Nicholas on the other. It would have sounded churlish to ask to be excused, even if she'd been able to extricate herself with ease. So she decided to make the best of it.

'Been shopping?' she asked conversationally.

Nicholas chewed for a moment.

'Sort of. Gemma was getting under Beth's feet, so I offered to take her into the town. And then Beth asked if I'd get her some embroidery silks, or tapestry wool, or something. She gave me a list of numbers, but I can't seem to find the darned shop anywhere. I don't suppose you——'

'Not really—sorry. I don't frequent that sort of shop. Have you tried the Brunel Plaza?' Tansy asked.

'That's an idea. We'll go there next, Gemma. What a good job we saw you. It's quite brightened up our day, hasn't it, Gemma?'

His grey eyes held Tansy's for a few seconds, and it was almost as though he was reading her thoughts, and knew just how much she really wanted him. She turned quickly away, embarrassed.

'We stopped to look at a wedding,' said Gemma.

'Was it a nice one? Where?'

'Christ Church,' said Nicholas. 'Don't gargle with your straw, Gemma.'

Gemma gave a defiant last bubble and put the glass down. 'It was a lovely wedding, Dr Tansy. She was all in white, and there were three bridesmaids all in pink, and a little boy in a skirt.'

'A kilt,' smiled Nicholas. 'A pageboy.'

'I'm going to be a bridesmaid,' Gemma announced.

'And when is that going to be?' asked Tansy, avoiding Nicholas's eye.

'I don't know when,' said Gemma guilelessly. 'But it will be when my daddy gets married, and I can have another mummy.'

Tansy could feel a lump in her throat. Nicholas looked angry.

'You're a chatterbox, Gemma,' he said gruffly. 'Come on, hurry up, we have to get Aunt Beth's silks.'

'I haven't finished my bun,' protested Gemma. 'But you did say that—I heard you. You told Aunt Beth I need a mummy.'

'Have you been listening at doors, young lady?' he demanded sternly.

'No, Daddy, you were in the kitchen with Aunt Beth, and I came back for my school book, and you——'

'I think we've heard enough. I was right, you do need someone to keep you in order. Aunt Beth spoils you.'

'So are you going to marry Dr Tansy, then?' persisted Gemma.

Tansy felt the hot colour creeping up her neck. 'I don't know where you got that idea from, Gemma. Your daddy and I are just friends. Aren't we, Nicholas?'

'Why don't you answer her question?' he asked instead.

'Because she didn't ask me. And I'm sorry, but I really have to go. I have to go to the library yet.'

'So aren't you coming to tea with us?' asked Gemma, quite unabashed.

'I have too much to do, Gemma,' Tansy said firmly. 'And really, you should have asked your daddy first.'

'But it was his idea when I saw you through the window.'

Nicholas coloured slightly. 'Well—yes, I did mention it. But you're right, it's very short notice.' He moved aside to let Tansy pass, and for a brief moment he rested his hand on her shoulder.

'I expect I shall see you in the hospital,' she murmured, feeling unaccountably shaken.

'Did you decide when you could see Gemma again?' he asked quietly.

She flushed guiltily. 'Oh—yes, I meant to tell you last night. I got sort of—sidetracked.' The memory of his kiss threatened to overwhelm her. 'I did check with my appointments book. Can you manage Tuesday, about two?'

'Sounds likely.'

'And could I talk to you first, to get some background information, do you think?'

'I'll be there. Beth can take her home.'

'Then that's settled.' She gave him a professional smile. 'Bye, Gemma.'

The child waved as she left the tea-shop, but Nicholas just watched her, not even smiling. The image of them standing there seemed to stay on Tansy's retina all day: Nicholas, tall and broad in his beige trench coat, light shining on his thick chestnut hair; Gemma, vivid in her red raincoat, her eyes darker than ever, her black hair sparkling from the rain. And she found herself wondering why it didn't seem right. She tried to imagine Beth standing there with them, tall, blonde, striking—but that wasn't right either. Then June, shorter, stockier, mousy hair in an old-fashioned style. That seemed even worse.

Beth looked the best, she decided. She'd be a good wife for Nicholas, and a good mother for Gemma. It was going to be very painful for herself, but if she made it clear there was to be no more of this unprofessional behaviour, he would realise she meant what she said, and would settle down with Beth.

It made sense, but it left her feeling sad and hollow inside.

CHAPTER EIGHT

TANSY settled herself comfortably and surveyed the people at the other side of the desk. The child reminded her a little of Debbie Ross, with her pale, mousy hair, light blue eyes behind owlish spectacles, but, more than these, her dejected, defeated air. A fearful child, she decided. Afraid of what?

Mrs Hinching was a thin, tight-lipped woman whose only sentiment towards her twelve-year-old daughter seemed to be disapproval. Mr Hinching, reluctantly squeezed into a chair too small for his eighteen-stone frame, hummed and haaed a lot, and seemed unable to meet Tansy's eye. Instead, he kept his gaze on her chest, which made her feel uncomfortable and awkward. He rarely looked at his wife.

The girl, Sarah, didn't resemble either of her parents. Perhaps Mrs Hinching's eyes were of a similar shape, but they were a sepia colour. And Mr Hinching's—when he raised his eyelids briefly—were like currants, black and beady. Of course, it was possible, brown-eyed parents could have blue-eyed offspring, but not vice versa. Tansy remembered her genetics.

Even so, she glanced again at Sarah's notes, while Mrs Hinching droned on about the way her daughter was bullied at school.

Name—Sarah Crosby. Age—— Crosby? How could she have overlooked this? Granted, she hadn't had much time to read the doctor's letter and the personal details in the file, but that was no excuse. She should have noticed the difference in the names.

She looked again at Mr Hinching, Sarah's stepfather. He had the appearance of a bully, perhaps a rather ineffectual bully, with his broad, heavy face, low-set ears, and shifty eyes. Tansy knew it was wrong to leap to such conclusions, but she couldn't help feeling there was something definitely unlikeable about him.

She turned her gaze to Mrs Hinching, who was fidgeting with her navy plastic handbag, talking in a whining voice about how she'd done everything for Sarah, and look how she'd repaid her.

Tansy murmured something non-committal. She turned to see if Mr Hinching agreed. But his gaze was on Sarah, a strangely intense stare, and Sarah seemed to be hypnotised by him. As Tansy spoke, the child's gaze dropped, and Mr Hinching smiled.

'How long has it been going on?' she asked, a feeling of disquiet growing in her. The parents exchanged fleeting glances. Co-ordinating their answers? thought Tansy.

'Her teacher told us six months ago. I was so embarrassed! That was the first time, and it was only a twenty-pence piece, but it was the little boy's bus fare, and he couldn't get home. You see, it was a new school, and I didn't want them to think——'

'A new school? Does she like the school?' asked Tansy.

'Well, it isn't the school she really wanted to go to. She took the exam for the Grammar School in Salisbury. She could have lived with her aunt during the week and come home weekends. But she failed, so she went to Churchfields instead. It's supposed to be a very good school, but I'm not sure. Perhaps Oakfield might have suited her better—it's smaller. Perhaps she's disappointed. Is that why you did it, Sarah? Is it?' demanded her mother.

Sarah cringed back in her chair, looking wildly from one person to another.

'Well, answer your mother, Sarah,' Mr Hinching put in, and nudged his stepdaughter.

'I don't know,' whispered Sarah. She looked like a little trapped rabbit.

'I'd rather you didn't question her, now she's coming to see me,' said Tansy smoothly.

Mrs Hinching snorted.

'She's really no need to do it—steal, I mean. She has everything she wants, good clothes—not second-hand, mind—good plain food, none of this junk stuff in packets, and a nice home, a lovely bedroom. What more can she want?'

'Love' was on the tip of Tansy's tongue, but she held it back.

'Does Sarah seem depressed to you?' she asked.

'Depressed? Can children get depressed?' said Mrs Hinching sceptically.

'Oh, yes. Anyone can get depressed if they have enough reason.'

Mrs Hinching snorted again. 'Sarah's got no reason to be depressed. No, of course she's not depressed. She's always been quiet—too quiet. But then I was never an outgoing child.'

Mr Hinching fidgeted in his seat, his face pink and moist.

'She was depressed,' he said unexpectedly. 'You remember, Freda. It was just before she started at her new school.'

'Well, *I* don't remember,' Mrs Hinching replied irritably. Tansy was aware of rising tension between them.

'Yes, you do. She used to cry at everything, every time we spoke to her. You remarked on it. You bought her a bottle of tonic. But she's better lately, Doctor.'

'Is she?' demanded Mrs Hinching. 'How can she be? It would have been better if she'd kept crying instead of taking to stealing. Now everybody will know!'

Tansy made a quick note to get Hattie involved. There was definite family disharmony here, and she suspected something more. She didn't like the way the stepfather watched the child—when he wasn't staring at her chest! Could there be—— It was an awful thought, but there was always a possibility. It was no good being hasty; look what had happened in other parts of the country when paediatricians—good paediatricians—had suspected this sort of thing wrongly.

She'd wait a while, and see. Sarah was twelve. She'd

tell her in her own good time. Tansy sent the Hinchings back to the waiting-room, and took Sarah across to the family dolls sitting on a shelf, the mothers, fathers, children. Sarah had an older brother, recently married.

'This could be Martin,' Tansy suggested.

Sarah took the doll and looked him over.

'I'm too old to play with dolls,' she said. But her gaze seemed drawn to a schoolgirl doll, in grey uniform. She put down the male doll and picked the other one up.

'She hasn't got glasses,' she commented, sitting the doll on a toy bed. Tansy watched and listened.

At Wednesday's meeting, Tansy told the others about Sarah Crosby, and her suspicions of the stepfather. Dan Rice frowned, and tapped his pen on the table.

'Be careful, Dr Blair,' he said quietly. 'Remember what happened in Cleveland.'

'I'm quite aware of that, Dr Rice,' she replied firmly. 'I shall be very careful not to ask loaded questions. I shall wait for an unmistakable indication from Sarah that something like that has been happening.'

'And you'll be very careful not to actually accuse the parents of what you suspect?'

'Naturally. If I do find abuse has been going on, I shall merely tell them Sarah's behaviour is indicative of this type of treatment, and ask if they can suggest where it may have happened.'

'You've done your homework well, Dr Blair. And if one of them actually admits to the abuse?'

'In that case I shall have to get other agencies involved. And I shall suggest therapy for the parents, family therapy and probably psychiatric therapy.'

'And where is the child while all this is going on?' asked Daniel.

'It may be necessary to place the child in care. Or, if the guilty person is agreeable, he himself could leave the home for treatment.'

'Preferable, I would have thought,' said Dan. 'Well, it seems you know the procedure for this sort of thing. But please remember not to rush into anything until you're sure. And let me know how things go on. I'm here to help and advise.'

His icy blue eyes held hers for a moment, and she flushed.

'Of course,' she murmured, and was relieved when Hattie mentioned Debbie Ross. Debbie and her parents had kept their appointment yesterday, and Tansy had been surprised to find Mr Ross a very likeable man, friendly and open, and very agreeable to anything Tansy suggested.

That was his problem, she had decided. He was agreeable to everything his wife suggested, even to leaving the entire upbringing of Debbie to her. When Tansy gave them her opinion that a daughter needed a male figure as a role model he seemed very surprised. Mrs Ross hadn't been quite so understanding.

'I never knew my father,' she stated, rather boastfully. 'My mother brought up all four of us girls on her own. And I'm sure you'll agree she made a very good job of it.'

Tansy made a tactful noise which Mrs Ross didn't appear to notice.

'She was a very dominant woman, my mother. I think it's good for a mother to be dominant, don't you?'

Tansy had smiled, and suggested that to a sensitive child like Debbie, dominance and authority was a little overpowering. It was going to be difficult persuading Mrs Ross to allow her daughter more autonomy and independence, but, given time, she was sure she could do it. In the meantime, it was important that Debbie knew someone understood her problems, and was on her side.

She told Hattie all this, and the family therapist agreed she would talk to the family, and try to change Mrs Ross's attitude to her husband and daughter.

Dan Rice glanced at his watch. Above him, the clock on the wall read four-twenty. The meeting had lasted longer than usual.

'Is that all?' he asked, looking round at everyone. There were murmurs of affirmation, and they all started to collect their files and papers, talking quietly between themselves.

'Do you think I can help in the Crosby case?' Hattie asked, as Tansy put her pen in her pocket.

'I'm sure you can, Hattie. But I'd like to put a few feelers out first, find out what the marital situation is really like. So far, I've just got Sarah's statement that they have lots of rows, and her mother doesn't always come off worst. If Mr Hinching does find it difficult to bully his wife, it could be he feels power over Sarah is a face-saving measure. Time will tell—Sarah's a bit resistant just now. But I'll certainly tell you, Hattie, because I'm sure you'll be needed.'

'Nice to know someone needs me!' joked Hattie, and went quickly after Ellen Chalmers, calling after her.

Dan had gathered his things together and was almost at the door when Tansy called out to him. He paused, and turned towards her, a closed look on his face.

'Yes, Tansy?' She noted that he only used her first name when they were alone together, and she wondered about it.

'Can you spare a few moments?'

'Is it a case, because if so you should have brought up the matter during the meeting,' he said curtly.

'It is—and it isn't. It concerns the child of a member of staff.'

He came back to the table and sat down, indicating that she should do the same.

'Please explain.'

Tansy found it difficult, with those pale blue eyes boring into her, so she told him only briefly about Nicholas and Gemma. It needed a great effort of will to stop her face giving herself away whenever she spoke of Nicholas, but Dan didn't appear to notice her reaction.

'So you've seen the child,' he said, when she had finished. 'Why didn't Dr Vernon come to me first? I am the chief.'

'Yes, I suggested it to him. He felt—he felt it needed a woman's touch. With Gemma losing her mother,' Tansy explained.

Dan frowned. 'I'm not sure that's his reason. But we'll skip it for now. Did you find the child disturbed?'

'She seems very confused about her mother's death. I feel she may have a misunderstanding of the situation. Nic—Dr Vernon insisted she doesn't know it was suicide, but I'm not so sure.'

She told him about the painting, and the coloured chalks that seemed to symbolise tablets. Dan shrugged.

'You may be right. On the other hand, it may mean nothing at all. Don't jump to conclusions. I find female psychiatrists do tend to jump to conclusions.'

'That's not fair!' Tansy replied hotly, her cheeks flushing with anger. 'I'm sure female psychiatrists are just as logical as male ones. And what you call jumping to conclusions is just another word for intuition. And, with experience, I'm certain intuition can be used efficiently.'

His keen blue eyes watched her reaction analytically. Was there a glint of amusement in them? Was he deliberately provoking her?

'And you feel you're experienced.'

'Quite experienced, yes,' she agreed. 'I've been working in child psychiatry for over three years now. I feel I know when to use logic and when to use intuition.' Why did she feel the need to defend herself? Daniel knew just how much experience she had.

'Ah, the famous intuition,' he said softly.

Tansy got up. 'I thought I might have had more understanding from someone with your reputation,' she said tartly, 'instead of this criticism of my character.'

'I'm sorry, I didn't mean to criticise. I was trying to give you some insight, but I went about it badly. Was I needling you?'

Tansy shuffled her feet. There was that look again in his eyes, that nakedness. It made her feel guilty, and that was stupid. She had gone to him for advice, and he had tried to intimidate her. She turned away from his gaze.

'Yes, you were needling me. Was there a reason?'

'No. No reason.' Dan's voice was so quiet she could hardly hear it, and she was strongly tempted to apologise for her own behaviour. Undecided, she sat again. He reached out and covered her hand with his lean, brown one.

'I'm sorry, Tansy, it's a bad habit I have. How can I make it up to you?'

'Please—you don't have to think like that. You're probably right. I do tend to act on hunches, call it what you like.' She snatched her hand away and picked up her bag. 'So it's all right if I continue to see Gemma?'

'Who? Oh, Dr Vernon's child. Yes, yes, of course you must see her. But it would be advisable to make some notes, have an official record of some sort. For your own protection,' Dan added.

'I'm already doing that. In case my memory fails me!' Tansy got up and started to walk away.

'Tansy.'

She paused, looked briefly over her shoulder at him.

'Did you have a nice evening last Wednesday?'

For a moment she wondered how he knew she had gone to Nicholas's home, and her cheeks reddened with embarrassment. Then she remembered the spare theatre ticket, and her inability to join him.

'Oh—last Wednesday—yes, I had a lovely time. Was the theatre good?'

'I didn't go. But I'm glad you enjoyed your evening.' He remained seated at the table, watching her. It seemed rather rude to walk away from him.

'I'm sorry. I have to go now——' she began.

'Another date, I expect.' But he was smiling, levering his long, bony frame out of the chair.

'Well——'

'You'd better hurry, then.' She flashed him a smile and almost scurried from the room. She hadn't handled that at all well! Perhaps she wouldn't make a good child psychiatrist, after all. Was she too impulsive, too emotional?

She hurried along to the Outpatients Department to collect her jacket.

When she returned to the department the next morning, she was accosted once again by Mrs Lawrence, dressed in an unseasonable fur fabric coat and bright scarf in gypsy fashion over her hennaed hair. Tansy thought quickly, recalled Pam's information that Désirée's appointment wasn't due yet, and paused to speak to the woman.

'Hello, Mrs Lawrence. How's Désirée?'

'Well, that's why I wanted to see you. She's having——'

'When is her next appointment, Mrs Lawrence?' asked Tansy.

'Oh, not for a month, Dr Blair, but I'm worried about her. She's not well, behaving quite strangely at times——'

'How do you mean?'

'Well, she's become very secretive, and she's not eating very well.'

'Is she on that diet I suggested?' Tansy was feeling unusually impatient. Mrs Lawrence was obviously prepared for a long talk, and there just wasn't time.

'I don't think so, Doctor. She's just off her food. And I——'

'If she's physically ill you must take her to your GP.'

'She doesn't like him much, Dr Blair. You're the only one she trusts. I know if I asked her to tell you what's bothering her, she would. Perhaps this afternoon——?'

'Mrs Lawrence, I'm afraid that's quite impossible. She should see her GP——'

'But I don't think it's physical,' said Mrs Lawrence triumphantly. 'I think she's going into an anxiety state again.'

The trump card. How could Tansy refuse? Sighing, she said, 'Tell the receptionist to fit her in next

Thursday, Mrs Lawrence. And I'm telling you now, I shan't be able to give her a full half-hour. I'm fully booked.'

'Of course, Doctor—I do realise that. You're very kind. Désirée thinks the world of you, you know.'

Smiling cheerfully now, Mrs Lawrence went across to the window, and Tansy could still hear her raucous voice persuading Pam to fit her in during the afternoon, as she went down to her office.

Tansy didn't seem to have much appetite. Like Désirée, she couldn't help thinking. Well, it wouldn't hurt the girl, she could lose two or three stones quite easily. But I can't! she argued.

She pushed away her half-eaten cottage pie, and took a mouthful of coffee. She glanced at her watch. Almost two o'clock. She hurried from the dining-room and back to her office.

Mrs Whitworth was already there with four-year-old Simon. He was playing with a toy tea-set, and his mother was reading a magazine. Tansy was pleased to see this. When Simon had first come to the hospital, at the age of two and a half, Mrs Whitworth had been worried out of her mind. Whatever he did, she had to supervise. She was afraid to leave him for a second in case he had a temper tantrum and held his breath.

The doctors had reassured her that he would always start breathing again within about half a minute, and if she remained calm the attacks would eventually stop. It had been a long, strenuous battle, but it had been won. This was his second visit to see Tansy, and would probably be his last.

She took them into the office with her, and Simon played with a toy lorry while Tansy hung up her jacket and put her bag in a drawer. Mrs Whitworth smiled happily, and Tansy knew the news would be good.

'How is he?' she asked.

'He starts school in September,' said Mrs Whitworth. 'Don't you, Simon?'

In response, the child brought the lorry across to show her.

'I'm learning to read, Dr Tansy,' he said, dangling the lorry by one wheel.

'He's very bright,' said Mrs Whitworth proudly. Suddenly the lorry fell to the floor. Tansy saw Mrs Whitworth tense, but she spoke calmly.

'Pick it up, Simon, there's a good boy.' She glanced at Tansy, and the doctor smiled. Mrs Whitworth had had to acquire a whole new set of reactions to Simon's behaviour. She'd learned how to leave him alone sometimes, to stop fussing and worrying, to keep calm. And it had worked.

'Any more breath-holding attacks?' asked Tansy, knowing what the answer would be.

'Oh, no, Doctor, not for the last six months.'

'No more temper tantrums?'

'Well, now and again, but nowhere near as bad as they used to be. He seems so much better now he's learning things. That was good advice you gave me.'

Tansy smiled. It hadn't been she alone. 'Do you think you need to bring him again?' she asked.

'I'm happy if you are, Doctor. And I think you've all done wonders with him.'

'We couldn't have done it without your help,' said Tansy.

Mrs Whitworth fumbled in her big brown handbag and came out with a small thin package in brown paper.

'This is for you,' she said awkwardly as she got up. 'For all you've done.'

'Oh, Mrs Whitworth—I've done hardly anything——' Tansy protested.

'Come along, Simon,' said his mother. 'Say goodbye to the doctor.'

'Goodbye, Dr Tansy.'

Tansy reached out and ruffled his reddish curls, almost the same colour as Nicholas's——

'Goodbye, Mrs Whitworth. Bye, Simon. Enjoy school!'

The door closed behind them. Tansy pushed the gift into a drawer. Now wasn't the time. Nicholas would be coming soon. And her heart started its usual racing. She wiped her damp palms on her oatmeal linen skirt, and pushed strands of bright hair off her forehead.

Ten minutes past two. He should be there. She went into the corridor and looked along to the waiting-room. And as she did so Nicholas and Beth came into view. They were talking earnestly, at least, Nicholas was, and Beth was nodding in agreement. Today she was wearing blue, and looked very much like the Beth doll Gemma had chosen. Blue suited her.

Tansy was about to turn away when Beth took Nicholas's face in her hands, and kissed him full on the mouth. And it was then that Tansy knew that Beth still loved him as much as she ever had. Then she disappeared from view, and Nicholas pushed open the door to the corridor. He saw Tansy standing there, and smiled.

'Where's Gemma?' she asked, without thinking.

'I thought you wanted to have a few words with me first.'

Oh, yes, yes, she wanted to say. Words, and words, and words. Enough words to keep you with me all day. She gave him a brief smile.

'I'm glad you've been able to find the time. I know you're busy.'

'My registrar is competent. He'll hold the fort until I get back. Gemma's with Beth.'

He followed her into the consulting-room, carefully moving the chairs so they were facing each other. He sat down and crossed his legs. She stood for a moment, disconcerted by his command of the situation.

'That violet colour suits you, Tansy. Matches your eyes.'

She refused to be drawn. 'Shall we begin?' she asked. She took Gemma's file from a locked drawer and sat down, relieved that her skirt wasn't short, and she had no ladders in her tights.

'We'll start from the beginning,' she said.

He smiled. 'Naturally.'

Tansy picked up her pen. 'Was her birth normal?'

He hesitated. 'Yes. Not instrumental, if that's what you mean.'

'Any serious childhood illnesses?'

'Only chickenpox when she was three.'

'Psychological problems?'

'Of course not! She's a sensible, intelligent, mature child.'

'Any problems with milestones? Teething, walking, talking?' Tansy went on.

'No. Look, Tansy, don't you think——'

'Any bedwetting?' she persisted.

A slight hesitation. 'Yes.'

Tansy wrote quickly, keeping her eyes on the paper in front of her, and wasn't aware of Nicholas's amused expression.

'Bedwetting. When did it start?'

'As soon as she was born until she was two and a half.'

Tansy began to write, frowned, and stopped. She looked up at him. He was grinning mischievously.

'Nicholas, this is very serious!' But she couldn't help it. She burst out laughing.

'Did you know you have a dimple—just there—when you laugh?' He leaned forward and touched her cheek gently. She resisted the urge to grab his hand and kiss it.

'Nicholas, will you please keep this on a professional footing? It's bad enough at other times, but this does happen to be a professional consultation.'

He pulled a face. 'I see—like that, is it? All right. What I've been trying to tell you is that Gemma is a perfectly normal little girl, and that's why her present disturbance is more upsetting. And I've been thinking over what you've said about it, and I'm inclined to go along with your theory of a misunderstanding over June's death. Where she's got it from, I can't say. But it does seem likely.'

'Do you still want me to see her, then? Or would you

like to work it out with her yourself? You were there when June died.'

'But you're the expert. I shall probably put my foot in it, say too much too soon. As far as I know, Gemma isn't aware of how her mother died. But I have no proof of this.'

'Then we'll take it from there,' she said quietly.

Nicholas stood up. 'And now I must go,' he said.

'Wait. There's a painting she did the other day. It puzzles me.' Tansy reached into the deep lower drawer of her desk.

'Perhaps another time?' Something about the way he stood, something sensual about him, stirred her senses. She found she was positively longing for him to take her in his arms again. To deny the feeling she shut the drawer angrily.

'I did expect you to stay longer, Nicholas. There's a lot we still haven't talked about—the basic data form, for a start.' She pushed it at him. 'To save time I suggest you fill it in yourself and let me have it next time.'

He took it, trying to hold her gaze. 'Don't I see you before then?'

'No, Nicholas, you don't. I'm sorry.'

For a moment he stood and looked at her, as if unable to accept what she had said. Then he put his hands on the desk.

'I can't imagine what I've done to warrant this anger from you, Tansy, this rejection of me, but don't think I shall run away with my tail between my legs, because I shan't.'

He walked towards the door and opened it. Tansy put her head in her hands. She heard the door close, then, surprisingly, footsteps approached the desk. She looked up suddenly, and was surprised to see a look of shocked horror on his face. But he came no closer, just stood and looked at her, and said, 'I shan't ask you what's wrong, Tansy. I'm hoping you'll tell me in your own time.'

'Please, Nicholas——'

'I came back because I think there's something you

should know. Personally, I don't feel it's anything to do with the case, but if you hear it from Beth, I shall be in hot water with you.' He sat down again, facing her. She opened the file.

'I don't want this recorded, Tansy. It's too private.'

'Is it family illness, Nicholas? I did wonder, when Beth was talking about her father, dying quite young——'

'Did she tell you?' he queried.

'Well, I'm afraid I have presumed rather,' Tansy admitted. 'I assumed she was George Gadsby's daughter. I don't know whether I'm right. But I do know he died quite young, in a psychiatric nursing home. It's common knowledge.'

Nicholas nodded. 'You guessed right. The girls were very young when he died.'

'A mental illness?'

'No, worse than that. Huntington's Chorea.'

CHAPTER NINE

TANSY couldn't answer for a moment. Her mouth felt dry. Nicholas's announcement had stunned her. When she looked at him he gave her a wry smile.

'Well, you wanted to know it all. I didn't want to tell you, but you forced my hand. June was sure she had Huntington's Chorea, and she couldn't face it.'

He was watching her closely. Tansy was only now feeling the full horror of what he had said.

'But—Huntington's is a dominant genetic——' she began.

He nodded. 'You're quite right, of course. And June had seen her father when he was very ill, and she couldn't bear the idea that she would suffer the same humiliating indignity of it all. You've seen Huntington's, I suppose?'

'A couple of times.'

'It's a degrading illness. June felt she couldn't face a future of increasing dependency on me—and Gemma eventually—and inevitable loss of mental faculties.'

'I'm beginning to understand,' murmured Tansy. It was not surprising that he and Beth avoided the subject whenever possible.

'She was quite wrong, of course,' said Nicholas in a calm voice. Tansy wasn't sure what he meant. She raised her eyebrows.

'There was no proof she had Huntington's Chorea,' Nicholas went on.

'Why wasn't she told?'

'She was—as far as it was possible to tell her. Oh, she had some symptoms, of course. She had episodes of depression, she was clumsy and nervous. But there was no absolute proof that it was Huntington's. She worked herself into an anxiety state, and that could have caused the symptoms. But we couldn't convince her. She thought we were hiding the truth from her.'

'Do you think it was Huntington's Chorea?' Tansy asked quietly.

Nicholas shrugged. 'Who knows? It was too early to tell. June told me then that ever since her early twenties she'd had it on her mind, waiting for the first signs. Even though her father was thirty-four when he began to suffer from it. It began to rule her life. I often wondered why she was so afraid to plan any long-term ventures. It was an obsession with her.'

'So no one knows whether she had it or not? Not even Dr Whittaker?'

'The symptoms were so mild. He did a few tests which gave doubtful results. So he was reluctant to give a definite answer until she gew worse. Bear in mind, that sort of diagnosis is not given lightly.'

Tansy sat back in her chair.

'You must have loved her deeply to agree to marriage with that disease in the family,' she said soberly, able to distance herself now from his problem.

'I didn't know when I married her.'

Tansy was shocked. 'Didn't anyone tell you?'

'Beth had gone to America. I married June quite quickly. It may seem strange to you now, but I did love her at first.' He seemed unable to meet her gaze, and his long fingers played with a calendar on the desk. 'I suppose after the wedding, her mother—whom we didn't see very often—must have assumed I knew about it. They occasionally talked about George Gadsby, who'd died in a mental hospital, but they never gave his illness a name, and from the signs it sounded rather like Alzheimer's Disease.'

'So who told you?' asked Tansy.

'Beth, when June sent for her. June was terrified of what she thought she'd got, and of telling me.'

'Yet you stayed with June to the end,' murmured Tansy.

'I married her. I took vows. HC or not, I had to stand by her. I'm made that way.'

He spoke simply, and Tansy felt a wave of love for him wash over her. She clenched her fists.

'Beth is her sister,' she said. 'So Beth has the same sword of Damocles hanging over her.'

Nicholas nodded. 'That's true. But Beth is much more stable. She would be able to take it.'

Confused emotions whirled inside Tansy's head. Why wasn't he bitter at June's deception? And why hadn't Beth told him all those years ago? A terrible realisation made her catch her breath.

'Nicholas, Gemma is June's daughter—that means if June did have HC, then Gemma could get it too! Didn't either of you think of this?' She knew it was an absurd question. He hadn't known about the HC six years ago. How could he possibly have forgiven June's family for allowing this to happen? Gemma could get HC! Gemma could get HC! The words ran around inside her head. Gemma. HC.

Nicholas rose from his chair. His expression was unfathomable. As he opened his mouth to say something, a sharp, high noise broke the silence. He switched off the bleep in his pocket and picked up the phone.

'Dr Vernon—you bleeped me. I see. Very well, I'll be right down.'

He strode to the door, pausing to look back at Tansy as he said, 'I've got to go to the Baby Unit—emergency. I hope what I've told you will go no further.'

He closed the door behind him, and Tansy sat frozen in her chair. What did he think she was? She was a trained doctor, she had taken the Hippocratic Oath. Did he think she would betray her oath of confidentiality and go blabbing to everyone that Nicholas Vernon had married into a family with Huntington's Chorea?

Suppressing her anger, she went out into the corridor and called Beth to bring Gemma. It must have been because of her new knowledge of the tragic disease in the Gadsby family that she found she was looking at Beth in

a new light. Despite Nicholas's asserting that Beth was
stable, and she could take it if it came to the worst, there
must have been times when she felt quite frightened
of her possible future. Although some valuable tests
had been developed to determine the presence of
Huntington's Chorea, there was still no immediate hope
of a cure.

So Beth was living under a terrible shadow, and she
must have been constantly aware of it. Every time she
dropped something, tripped up, forgot something
important, or felt depressed, the awful fear must cross
her mind. Was this the beginning?

And it was this dreadful anxiety that had killed her
sister. Perhaps not the disease itself. So, as Beth
approached her, holding Gemma's hand, Tansy found
herself casting a professional eye over her face. She
didn't look depressed, just as disdainful as usual as her
bright blue eyes swept over Tansy's figure.

Tansy had had a busy morning, and a late, rushed
lunch. She was aware that she probably looked a little
untidy, a mite windswept. But right now it didn't
concern her, she was too determined to feel sorry for
Beth, in spite of her glamour and her expensive clothes.

'Shall I wait?' Beth asked as they met.

'You can go home, Aunt Beth,' said Gemma gaily. 'If
I'm going to play in Dr Tansy's room I shall be here
until Daddy comes.'

Tansy laughed. 'I'm sorry, Gemma, not this time, I'm
afraid. I have some——' she hesitated '—some other
children to see later.'

Gemma looked crestfallen, so she added quickly, 'But
you can stay until three o'clock. All right?'

'Oh, all right.'

'Half an hour, then,' said Beth. 'I'll do some meditation.' She walked easily back to the waiting-room, her
hips swinging in the slim-fitting blue dress.

Meditation, thought Tansy. That's not a bad idea. I
could do with some. She smiled down at Gemma and
took her hand.

'Are we painting?' asked Gemma, as they went into the office.

Tansy slipped off the child's denim jacket and hung it on a hook.

'No, not today, we haven't time. What about setting up the dolls' house? See, you can take the front off.'

She demonstrated, revealing the six rooms within, all empty. She turned to Gemma, who was standing in the middle of the floor, looking puzzled.

'Come on, Gemma,' she said gently.

'You didn't come to our house again, Dr Tansy.'

'I wasn't asked. And I'm a very busy person.'

'But I've come to see you, when I should be at school. Aren't you too busy today?'

Tansy tried to find a suitable excuse, but Gemma said quickly, 'Is it because I'm a patient now?'

'Do you think you're a patient?' queried Tansy. 'Are you ill?'

'Not now. Not since I was sick on my birthday. But I heard Daddy and Aunt Beth talking, they're always talking together.'

Tansy felt a wrench at her stomach, but she kept smiling.

'And what were they saying?' she asked.

'Aunt Beth said she thought I'd get better on my own, but Daddy said he wanted you to help.' She knelt in front of the dolls' house and opened the windows.

'Do you want me to help?' asked Tansy softly, kneeling beside her.

'Help me to do what? I thought patients had to be ill. I don't feel ill.' Gemma placed a bed in one of the bedrooms.

'No, of course you don't. It's not that sort of illness that I deal with. I help children who are upset or worried. Perhaps they're not happy at home, or at school.'

Gemma put a doll on the bed and covered it with a tiny blanket.

'I like school,' she said, without looking at Tansy.

'That's good. Some children are unhappy because their mummies or daddies have left them. Or have died.'

The whole hospital seemed to be still. Tansy was sure she could hear her own heartbeat.

'My mummy left me,' said Gemma, and sat another doll on a chair in the bedroom. Tansy felt it was strange that she had phrased it that way. Left her? Not died?

'Your mummy died,' she said gently.

'No, she left me. I heard them talking about it. They said she'd gone for an operation, but she didn't tell me about it, and anyway I saw her, and she was all yellow, and she wouldn't wake up, and I expect she'd had a sleeping tablet, a blue one, but then Aunt Beth went up, and they took her away, and they said—but it wasn't true—they told lies——'

The little girl's face was crumpling, her fingers twisting in distress. 'They said the operation had killed her, but I know it wasn't true!'

Her cheeks were flushed, her pansy eyes full of tears. Tansy gently drew her close, and she collapsed against her, sobbing convulsively as her fears surfaced. After a few minutes, Tansy gently wiped her moist face and stroked her dark curly hair.

'How did you know it wasn't true?' she asked softly.

It was just as she had imagined. Gemma had overheard something and had misunderstood it. And in some way she felt guilty. Had she wished her mother dead, during a fit of pique? Most children did. And Gemma's next words confirmed her ideas.

'I told you,' said Gemma, moving furniture in the house, 'I heard them talking. And they said she'd done something—a funny word—sudsi—sudi—something—I don't know what it means.'

'Suicide?'

'That's it. And then Aunt Beth said she wasn't surprised that Mummy had killed herself. But, Dr Tansy, I know she didn't kill herself, because I killed her, so she had to leave me.'

She spoke in a flat voice, and Tansy listened in horror.

Gemma knew about the suicide, if not the word, but something in her couldn't believe her mother would deliberately choose to leave her, so she had made up her mind it was her own fault. Something she had said or done had caused her mother to die.

Tansy wasn't sure how she was going to convince her otherwise. And perhaps now wasn't the time to start. She deliberately placed a dining table in the middle of the hall. As she expected, Gemma promptly removed it and put it in the dining-room.

Tansy glanced at her watch. Five to three. Perhaps this was the time for Gemma to go. She stood up, brushing fluff from her tights.

'Would you like to come again, Gemma?' she asked.

'Can't you come to my house?' queried the child.

'It's very difficult in the daytime, as I'm so busy. And in the evenings I expect you're in bed.'

'But I'm not asleep!' Gemma denied hotly. 'You could talk to me while I'm in bed.'

'No, I think you'd be too tired.'

'Do you work Saturdays and Sundays?'

Tansy laughed. Gemma was a most determined child, she decided. And a wily little monkey! She ruffled her hair.

'I'm not sure your daddy and Aunt Beth want me around at weekends.' She fetched Gemma's jacket.

'I think Daddy would. I heard him talking——'

'Please! No more!' laughed Tansy. 'I have an awful feeling you listen at keyholes, young lady. And that's not a nice thing to do.'

'I don't—honestly!' Gemma pushed her arms into the sleeves. 'I come downstairs when I'm supposed to be asleep, and they leave the doors open, and I hear them. I only come down for a glass of milk, but they don't hear me.'

'I see. Well, come along. Aunt Beth is waiting.'

'She cried when Mummy went away,' said Gemma calmly. Tansy decided not to go into that. She couldn't imagine Beth crying, losing control. Perhaps she was

misjudging her. Perhaps all that meditation had trained
her to appear calm and untroubled.

Beth was reading a magazine in the waiting-room. She
put it down when she saw Gemma.

'All right?' she asked the child, not looking at Tansy.

'I played with the dolls' house,' said Gemma. 'Do I
have to go back to school today, Aunt Beth?'

'Not much point now, dear. Shall we go and have a
milkshake in the town?'

'Oh, yes! Bye, Dr Tansy.'

At last Beth turned and looked at Tansy. 'Does she
have to come again?' she asked.

'There are one or two things that need sorting out,'
said Tansy slowly. 'Could you bring her at four-thirty
next Tuesday?'

'Of course. Whatever you say.' Beth took Gemma's
hand and they left the department. Tansy gazed after
them, then went back to her office. As she opened a desk
drawer to replace Gemma's notes, her fingers encoun-
tered a small parcel. Mrs Whitworth, she remembered.
Smiling, she pulled off the wrapper. Inside was a silver-
plated ballpoint pen engraved with her name. But it had
been spelled wrong: TANSEY. She shrugged. It would
still write. She put it in her pocket.

The last patient of the day hadn't yet arrived when Tansy
ushered out Mrs Wilkinson and her five-year-old mute
son, Errol. It was their second visit, and Tansy knew it
would probably be some time before he would speak to
her, or to anyone else except his mother. Elective mutism
always presented a challenge, but the results were usually
good, particularly in children of Errol's age. He had
talked normally before starting school, but since then he
had spoken to no one except his mother. Tansy was
planning to start behaviour therapy, as she had used this
before with success. But if it didn't work there would
always be special play therapy, and even persuasion and
coercion.

The door closed behind them, and she glanced at the

clock. Four forty-five. And no one in the waiting-room. Where was Sharon Carless? Tansy went back to her room and re-read the report from the GP. Sharon was thirteen, and had had pains in her legs for a few months, with no apparent organic cause. Rightly, her doctor had felt it might be psychosomatic, and Tansy was inclined to agree. Pain was a very subjective thing. But where were Sharon and her mother? Had they cancelled, and she hadn't been told? She went back to the reception office to ask Pamela, and, as she reached the waiting-room, the far door was pushed open by a porter wheeling in a pretty, smiling, dark-haired girl, followed by a worried-looking woman in a black raincoat and yellow headscarf.

As Tansy moved to meet them, the girl said, 'Hello. I'm Sharon Carless.'

Surprised, Tansy murmured, 'Hello, Sharon. Glad you could get here.'

'The ambulance was late,' complained Mrs Carless, as Tansy took the handles of the wheelchair and began to wheel the girl down the corridor. Pains in the legs? So bad she was unable to walk? She didn't appear to be in pain. Could the GP have made a mistake?

Mrs Carless held open the door of the office. Once they were all settled, Tansy said, 'I'm Dr Blair, usually called Dr Tansy by the children. I'm sorry, but I wasn't told Sharon couldn't walk. Is the pain very bad, Sharon?'

But Sharon was gazing around the room with interest, her bright, intelligent eyes taking in every detail. Her face showed no sign of stress.

'Pain, Doctor? No, she doesn't have any pain,' said Mrs Carless. 'Do you, Sharon? No, sort of paralysed they are. Not all the time. Just now and again.'

Puzzled, Tansy read again the handwritten letter from the GP. Pains in the legs—oh no, his writing was so bad—not pains, but paralysis.

Sharon smiled happily at her, and Tansy knew immediately she was dealing with a case of conversion disorder. In other words, hysteria.

* * *

It was almost half-past five by the time Tansy had finished her interview with Sharon. As she passed the appointment card to Mrs Carless, her bleep went. She switched it off and picked up the phone.

'Tansy? It's Nicholas. I'm in Casualty.'

Tansy was puzzled, to say the least. And she hoped Mrs Carless and Sharon hadn't noticed the flush that instantly flooded her cheeks.

'Casualty?' she echoed. 'It—it isn't Gemma, is it? Has she had an accident?'

She knew the words were foolish even as she uttered them. Why should he inform her if Gemma had had an accident? She wasn't a surgeon. She glanced at her watch.

'Oh, no, Gemma's fine, as far as I know. Tansy, I've got a child here, a girl of ten, presenting with very strange symptoms, and I've ruled out any physical cause as far as I can at this stage. I suppose some blood biochemistry might reveal something, but that will take time. I'd like you to look at her.'

'Any idea what——?' she began.

'None at all. Never seen anything like it before. Will you? I'm sorry it's so late, but she seems to be out of my province, and I'm not sure whether I ought to admit her or not.'

'I'll be down as soon as I can. Ten minutes.' Tansy put down the receiver. Mrs Carless and Sharon were waiting expectantly.

'Sorry about that. I've got to go to Casualty,' said Tansy. 'But I'll see you next week, Sharon, and we'll talk again.'

'Won't she have to be admitted, Doctor?' asked Mrs Carless. Sharon looked eagerly at her.

'Not today, Mrs Carless,' said Tansy, and Sharon looked sulky.

'What if I can't walk next week?' she asked belligerently.

'Then we'll talk again, and I'm sure we'll soon get to the bottom of it.'

Mrs Carless opened her mouth to protest, but Tansy forestalled her. 'I'll arrange for a porter and an ambulance to take you home, Mrs Carless. If you'll just wait there for a little while.'

The porter quickly arrived, and they all disappeared along the corridor, Sharon insisting plaintively that she just knew she'd never walk again, and Mrs Carless telling the porter that some doctors just didn't know what they were talking about.

Tansy sighed. She'd have been appreciated more if she'd taken up medicine or surgery, she felt. It was easier for patients to understand something they could see. She quickly wrote in Sharon's file, picked up her jacket and bag, and left the department.

Casualty didn't appear to be very busy. Two nurses chatted at the reception desk, two middle-aged women sat on the hard plastic chairs eating potato crisps, a scruffy young man with a tangled beard was trying to get Coke from the machine without money, shaking the offending dispenser frustratedly. One of the nurses went across to remonstrate with him.

Tansy looked around for Nicholas, and, as though he knew she had arrived, he appeared around the cubicle curtains at the far end of the row. At the same time, Tansy was aware of a high, thin, keening sound. A child weeping hopelessly. Her heart went out to her.

Nicholas looked pleased to see her. 'You weren't long,' he said.

'I'd just finished with a patient. Where is she?'

'Do you want to see her first, or shall I give you all the facts? The Casualty Officer saw her first, took some notes, not sure what to do with her, rang me, ditto. But I did take the notes in more detail.'

'You'd better tell me then. Forewarned is forearmed.'

'What about in here?' He drew back the curtains of the nearest cubicle. 'We shan't get disturbed.'

Tansy couldn't prevent the little shiver that ran through her as she passed him and pulled out the small bench provided for visitors. Nicholas drew the curtain across and sat beside her. He opened the file.

'You smell nice,' he said softly, and she swallowed.

'Can we get on? It's late.'

He gave her a quick sideways glance. 'Certainly. Her name is Emily—Emily Davis. The woman in the cubicle with her is her foster-mother, Mrs Walsh. She gave Dr Lewis the basic history. Emily's mother, Heather Davis, had a brief affair with a Pakistani boy when she was sixteen, and Emily was the result. Heather stayed with the child for three years, a squalid bedsit, by all accounts. Lots of one-night stands, according to Mrs Walsh. I don't know if it's true. Well, one day Heather took Emily to nursery and never picked her up—went off with another man. Emily was in care for a while, then fostered until she was five, when her mother came back, convinced the authorities she was in a stable relationship with someone called Dean—not the one she'd gone away with.

'Things were reasonable for a while. Heather managed to get a council flat. Emily was at school. Then Heather took a part-time job in a café, and a neighbour with children used to collect Emily every afternoon from school, with her own. Things seemed to be settling down. One day—the old story—Heather didn't come for her. Dean had gone too, but not with Heather, it seems. Emily was brought to Mrs Walsh. She was seven—three years ago. Mrs Walsh insists there have been no problems——'

'No problems? With that history?'

'I queried that when I spoke to her. The woman's very much on the defensive, Tansy, I'm not sure if she's hiding something.'

'At the very least the child must be insecure. Did you notice many signs of that?'

'It was difficult to examine her. She's like a frightened rabbit—that high wailing sound you can hear, like a rabbit in a trap. I couldn't be sure whether she had any physical pain or not. I don't think she does. She just seems terrified.'

'Of the foster-mother?' asked Tansy.

'Of everyone.'

'What made her like this? Why did Mrs Walsh bring her here?'

'I think because she got scared herself. She couldn't quieten the child. She made sure I knew she'd fostered over forty children, and no problems with the others. I took that with a pinch of salt.'

'Is there a Mr Walsh?' asked Tansy.

'He's a factory worker, works shifts. She assured me he was like a father to them all, and they loved him. She was on the defensive.'

'Are we going to get involved in something, Nicholas?' Tansy wanted to know.

'I certainly hope not.' He tapped his pen on the paper. 'I didn't see any signs of it, Tansy. I think Mrs Walsh is just plain scared of losing her livelihood.'

'Then why is Emily so terrified?'

Nicholas shrugged. 'I just can't figure it out. I can't get any response from her except the wailing. I can only go by what Mrs Walsh told me.'

He turned and looked at her, and she had a sudden urge to kiss him.

'And what was that?'

He checked his notes. 'The Walshes live in Dudmore Road. Emily—and two other children at the house— attend Drove Junior School. Emily came home from school today and wanted to watch television. Mrs Walsh said she had to change her clothes and wash first. Emily had a bit of a tantrum, and Mrs Walsh took her upstairs herself, and put her in the bathroom. She was gone a long time, then there was an awful scream, and Mrs Walsh found her standing in the empty bath looking terrified. Eventually she managed to get a bath towel round the child, and a neighbour offered to bring them here in the car.'

'And there's no physical injury?' asked Tansy.

'None that I can see. But I can't send her home like this, Tansy. She just squats there and shudders, like someone who's had a shock. She doesn't say anything except, Not Emily, Not Emily.'

'Not Emily?' Tansy looked at him. 'What do you think that means?'

He shrugged. 'I have no idea.' Their eyes met. 'You look tired,' he said softly.

'No, Nicholas, this isn't the time or the place. The child, Emily——'

'I merely said you look tired, Tansy. You work too hard. You need a holiday.'

'In case you've forgotten, I've just had one. Now, Emily——'

'And you came back looking sad and hurt. I noticed it, Tansy, that day I met you in the corridor, last week— Tuesday. I wanted to hold you, Tansy, and kiss the pain away——' He grasped her hand. Tansy could feel a pulse throbbing deep inside her. She pulled her hand away and stood up.

'I'd better see Emily. The end cubicle?'

'What's wrong, Tansy?' he persisted. 'Can't you tell me?'

'Nothing's wrong.' She drew back the curtain. A nurse walked past, glancing curiously inside. Nicholas stood behind her.

'That's right. At the end. When——' His bleep made her jump. He crossed to reception to use the phone. Tansy watched him, a deep sadness inside. Was this what the rest of her life was going to be like? Did she have to be such a coward, because of what Rod had done to her?

She put on a smile and entered Cubicle Eight. The child, a thin, dark-haired girl with big brown eyes, and legs like coffee-coloured matchsticks, sat huddled at the top end of the couch, her arms around her knees.

Mrs Walsh, a big, raw-boned woman with a high colour and frizzy blonde hair, sat looking at her, red plastic handbag on her knees. She stood up when Tansy came in, but didn't speak.

'Hello, Mrs Walsh,' said Tansy brightly. 'Hello, Emily.'

'Not Emily,' muttered the child, and began the high-pitched whining.

'For God's sake stop that noise,' said Mrs Walsh irritably. 'You're giving me a headache!' Emily ignored her, and she turned to Tansy. 'Have you seen him? The doctor? What does he say?' she demanded. Her hostile eyes eyed Tansy's well-cut oatmeal suit, the amethyst brooch on the lapel.

'He doesn't feel she's physically ill——'

'Then what's she howling for? Anybody'd think I'd belted her one. I've never laid a finger on her!'

'I'm sure you haven't, Mrs Walsh,' said Tansy gently.

'Well, is he going to keep her in? Did he tell you?'

'That will be up to me, Mrs Walsh. If I agree her problem seems to be psychological——'

'Up to you? Aren't you a social worker?'

'No, I'm a child psychiatrist.'

'A doctor? Where's your white coat?' Mrs Walsh seemed to be blaming Tansy for her own misunderstanding. Tansy smiled.

'I don't wear one—white coats tend to frighten children. And Emily already seems frightened enough.'

The child's crying had abated, and she was casting frequent sidelong glances towards her.

'Just standing in the empty bath, not a stitch on,' Mrs Walsh muttered. 'Well, it's not natural. What's come over her?'

'I hope I can find out,' said Tansy. 'Now I'd like to talk to her alone, Mrs Walsh, so if you could wait in the waiting-room——'

'Psychiatrist, you said. It's in her head? She's insane?'

'That's a strong word, Mrs Walsh. But she's suffered a lot of trauma in her life.'

Mrs Walsh nodded. 'That's true. Not surprised she's flipped her lid. Some of the things she's said!'

'What sort of things?' queried Tansy.

'Well, not to me, you understand—to herself. Muttering. Words, threats, "gonna kill you"—things like that. Wicked things. I expect she's like her mother—a bad lot.'

'You shouldn't say things like that, Mrs Walsh. Now, if you could leave us alone, I'll call you when I've finished.'

'I'd better get meself a cup of tea,' grumbled Mrs Walsh, as she left the cubicle. Tansy sat on the end of the couch, and Emily stared at her.

'Well, we are in a pickle, aren't we?' Silence. 'Come on, Emily, I know you can talk. You are Emily, aren't you?'

The child opened her mouth, prepared to wail, but Tansy said quickly, 'All right, you're not Emily. Let's leave it at that.'

Emily stared at her, but appeared to relax slightly.

'Do you like school?' Tansy asked. 'I bet you play hopscotch—you know, where you chalk out a circle, with six——'

'It isn't a circle! It's ten squares.'

Tansy smiled. 'So it is. All right. Who do you play hopscotch with?'

'Jane.'

Tansy tried not to show her exultation.

'How old is Jane?'

'Seven.'

'I see. She's a lot younger than you.'

'No. I'm a week younger than Jane.'

'You're seven?' Tansy felt stirrings of excitement. This was one case she'd never met before.

'Where do you live, Emily?' she asked gently.

'Bonnie! I'm not Emily, I'm Bonnie.' Her voice changed, became shrill. 'Gonna kill you, Bonnie! You'll wish you'd never bin born! Gonna kill you, Bonnie!'

Her eyes were wide and dark with terror. Tansy put out a hand and took hers. She didn't protest.

'Who's going to kill you, Bonnie?'

'Heather! Gonna kill Bonnie!'

'What happened today, Bonnie?' The child shuddered, and moved imperceptibly nearer.

'Went to school. Patty fetched me. Played in her flat. Had bread and jam. A policeman came—and Eileen. I don't like Eileen. I went to the bathroom for a wee, but it was a different colour! A yellow bath! I went and I—looked outside—and there were stairs! I don't know where I am! Where's Patty? Where's Patty?'

Tansy gently wiped the sweat from the child's face.

'Bonnie, I'm not quite sure what's happened. But something upset you, and you forgot where you were. And now you live at Mrs Walsh's house, and she looks after you. Would you like to go home now?'

Tansy didn't intend that Emily/Bonnie should be at home, but she wanted to see her reaction. She pulled back the curtains and beckoned Mrs Walsh to come into the cubicle. The woman walked up to the couch.

'Feeling better, Emily?' she asked brightly. Emily/Bonnie cowered back with terrified eyes.

'What shall we do, Bonnie?' asked Tansy gently.

'Bonnie? Her name's Emily,' said Mrs Walsh, puzzled.

'She's Bonnie. And she's seven. And she's waiting for Heather to collect her from Patty's house.'

'Flat,' said Emily/Bonnie automatically. Mrs Walsh looked aghast.

'She's talked, then?'

'She's told me a lot. She's very upset. I asked her if she wanted to go home with you.'

'That's right,' said Mrs Walsh soothingly, taking Emily/Bonnie's arm.

The child flung herself away, crying, 'No—no—no! Kill me—kill Bonnie—all kill Bonnie—hurt her—don't like the strap——'

Mrs Walsh stepped back, looking thunderous.

'I don't know what she's talking about. I've never laid a finger on her. You're telling lies, Emily Davis, you're being a very naughty girl, and you know what happens to naughty girls. The policeman will come——'

'Please, Mrs Walsh! That's enough! Can't you see how upset she is?' Emily/Bonnie was crouched on the couch, her hands over her ears, her eyes closed. Tansy moved towards her, breathing hard. She was beginning to get a clear picture of the situation.

'I think you'd better go home, Mrs Walsh,' she said firmly. 'Bonnie can stay here overnight until we find out what's bothering her.'

'Will she come home tomorrow?' the woman asked. 'I suppose I shall have to tell the social workers, and they won't be pleased. They'll blame me.'

'I can't help that, Mrs Walsh. Why don't you ring the hospital tomorrow, and we can tell you more.'

'How am I going to get home? Mr Howard's gone. Can someone get me an ambulance?'

'It isn't late, Mrs Walsh. I'm sure you'll get a bus not far from here,' Tansy told her.

'She's an ungrateful little minx. After all I've done for her!' Muttering, the woman left the cubicle, and Tansy deftly drew up a syringe of a mild sedative. Emily/Bonnie hardly resisted as it was given, and soon lay sleeping on the couch. Tansy covered her with a blanket. Then, leaving a nurse with her, she made arrangements to admit her to the ward. She sat by the desk, feeling incredibly weary.

Soon Emily/Bonnie was tucked up in bed in the ward, and Tansy sat in the office, writing up the notes. A shadow fell across the desk. She looked up.

'Hello, Tansy.'

'Dr Rice! I've just admitted a little girl with apparent loss of memory. I haven't met anything quite like it before, and I've got a feeling she might well be a case of multiple personality. I know it's just a hunch and I know what you think about hunches, but I'm sure——'

'It's not impossible, Tansy. Multiple personality—it happens. And I trust your judgement. You haven't made any mistakes yet.'

She flushed. 'She's ten, but she thinks she's seven. She couldn't understand why she found herself in a strange house. Her name's Emily, but she calls herself Bonnie. She——'

'I'll read the notes, Tansy. We can discuss it at next week's meeting.' Dan sat near the desk, watching her. She felt very self-conscious as she finished writing. Dan didn't speak. Finally Tansy closed the file and asked awkwardly, 'Was there something you wanted to see me about?'

'You? Oh, no, I came to see Gerald Macey. He had another epileptic attack today, and I shall have to reconsider the diagnosis of acute anxiety. I shall arrange for a CAT-scan as soon as possible.'

'You think a brain lesion?' asked Tansy.

'Very likely. But the headaches have only been recent.'

Tansy was tired. She'd had a hard day, and it was after seven o'clock. She tried to subdue a yawn, but Dan noticed it.

'You look tired, Tansy,' he said quietly.

'I've had a long day. I shall be all right once I've had a meal and a long soak.' She tried to appear alert.

'You're conscientious,' he told her. 'You'll do very well, as long as you don't overdo it. And as long as some man doesn't run off with you and marry you.'

His icy blue eyes watched her steadily, and she felt embarrassed.

'There's no chance of that. I want a career.'

His eyes narrowed. 'Is that why you chose children for your speciality?'

'I don't understand.'

'You don't intend to marry and have a family,' Dan stated curtly, his blue eyes probing. 'But your natural instincts are to nurture children. Is it just the thought of a husband that puts you off?'

'It's nothing like that at all, Dr Rice! And it's no business of yours, or anyone else's, so please stop trying to analyse me!'

'I wasn't aware—oh, well, it's probably a natural

instinct with me. Particularly when I meet someone who has so much to offer, yet she chooses to isolate herself from all the good things in life.'

Tansy turned on him angrily. 'Isn't that a matter of opinion, the good things in life? And I could ask the same questions of you, Dr Rice! Why are you unattached? And why did you choose paediatrics?'

He winced visibly. 'Touché! I deserved that, Tansy. Look, can I make amends? Come and have dinner with me tonight, at my flat.'

Warning bells sounded in Tansy's head. She sensed that the invitation had not been given without some thought. If he were serious about her, then it would not be fair to let him assume she liked him in that way.

'Thank you, Dan, but no.' Her voice was quiet but resolute. He looked at her for a moment, but his pride prevented him from pleading. He straightened his shoulders.

'Very well.'

'I appreciate your offer,' she said. He gave her a crooked smile and left the office. Tansy stretched back in her chair, and her blouse pulled against the swell of her breasts. She yawned, and stretched again, her violet eyes closed.

'Ahem!' She jumped, and turned. Nicholas stood inside the door, watching her. She straightened her jacket.

'Don't do that, Nicholas! You made me jump.' He came and stood behind her, and one hand gently but sensuously stroked the top of her breast. She pulled away instinctively, then relaxed, and leaned her head against him. This was bliss, but it was no use——

'Nicholas, you shouldn't be doing this,' she murmured. 'I'm too tired to resist. You've got me at a disadvantage. I was just going home to bed.'

'Yes, please,' he murmured. She stirred in the chair. Her emotions were so near the surface, and she wanted so much to agree to his suggestion. Then she had a vision of Rod, laughing Rod, at the house in Wiltshire, the police bringing the news, Christina Swallow——

'Nicholas, you're making it impossible for me,' she sighed. 'Go away!'

'It's not impossible. It's the easiest thing in the world. I love you, Tansy—there, I've said it! I love you. I want to marry you.'

She stood up and faced him, his arms still holding her close.

'But you hardly know me,' she murmured weakly.

'I don't need to. That will come later.'

'No!' She jumped away from him. 'Don't you see, later will be too late!'

'I don't see that at all. Tansy——' Nicholas pulled her into his arms again, 'have I been wrong to imagine you feel something for me?'

'No—no—Nicholas, it's no use. You don't know me, and if you did know me you'd leave me alone.'

'Why, have you got some dreaded plague? You don't look ill. Just tired.'

Tansy giggled. She was beginning to feel hysterical, and whoever heard of a hysterical psychiatrist?

'Of course not—nothing like that. Nicholas, if you knew me any better, you wouldn't like me. I just know that.'

'Well, I'm sure you're not a murderer, so there can't be anything worse in your life. You can't have killed a patient—you'd have been struck off. And you're too good for that. Tansy, I love you now, this minute; I don't care what happened in your past.' He held her away from him. 'Is that what bothers you so much? Something you did before you came to Greenstead? Because if so, I don't care. I just don't believe you've ever done a wicked thing in your life. It isn't in you. Tansy, I can see it, I feel it when I kiss you, you have such a lot of love to give. How about giving some of it to me?'

CHAPTER TEN

TANSY looked at him, her lower lip trembling. It would be so easy, just to say she loved him, never to talk about what had happened six years ago, and Rod—— No, she couldn't do it. To be free to love again, she had to be free of the past. Yet, because of that past, she could never be free.

There was a tap at the door behind them, and they jumped apart. The little red-haired nurse's glance flickered over them.

'I'm sorry, Dr Blair, I thought Sister was here——'

'I think she went to supper,' said Tansy. 'Can I help?' Inwardly, she couldn't help thinking, This is going to start a rumour, and she glanced at Nicholas.

'I shouldn't think so. Scott and Toby are asking for the Monopoly. I suppose that's a good sign, isn't it? But I can't find it anywhere.'

'Did I see it on top of this cupboard? Ah, here it is.'

'Oh, thanks, Dr Blair. Sorry to have—er—barged in like that.'

'Don't mention it.' Yes, there was certainly going to be more news on the grapevine! The nurse hurried away, closing the door behind her. There were faint whoops of excitement from the ward.

'Where were we?' asked Nicholas.

Tansy picked up her bag, and suppressed a yawn. 'I don't know about you, but I'm going home.' She was afraid to look at him. Perhaps it was the exhausted state she was in, perhaps a subconscious need for closeness, but as she turned from the desk her foot caught in the chair and she stumbled. Nicholas's reaction was rapid, as he grabbed her arm and drew her to him.

'I seem to make a habit of this, don't I?' she murmured, but she couldn't deny the safety she felt in his arms. Safe, secure. . .

'It's quite an endearing habit,' he assured her. 'As long as I'm around.'

'I'm quite all right—I can walk.'

'Doesn't matter. If you can't I shall carry you.'

'Promises, promises!' she teased, trying to appear light-hearted.

'All right, if you don't believe me.' He swept her off her feet as though she were a child, and she let out a little cry.

'Nicholas, this is a hospital! Put me down! What do you think you're doing? Anyone might come in.'

'I don't care. I shall put you down on one condition.'

'I don't make bargains. I told you that once before.' Or had she? She couldn't remember. His face was very close. A pulse beat in his neck.

'Come and have a meal with me.'

'I'm not hungry.'

'You're just saying that. I shall cook it for you—roast duck with orange, baby potatoes, green peas, white wine.'

Against her will, her mouth was watering. 'All right. How can I resist?'

Nicholas lowered her to the floor, and she straightened her skirt. She was breathing quickly. Couldn't he see the effect he had on her?

'Come on then. Grab your bag.' He took her hand, and they hurried through the quiet corridors, and out of the hospital.

'We'll take my car,' he said decisively. 'Firstly, because I don't like being driven. Secondly, because I know the way. Thirdly, you're far too tired, and I'm not going to risk an accident.' He unlocked his Mercedes, and they took their seats. 'Although, if you didn't have your car for a while, I'd be forced to chauffeur you everywhere, wouldn't I? And that could have its advantages.' He started the engine, and they moved away. Tansy hadn't really been aware of his words. They seemed to wash over her as they drove along. The car was so comfortable, it would be so easy just to fall asleep. She closed her eyes.

But why had he stopped so suddenly? She looked through the window. This wasn't Swindon! This was somewhere she'd never seen before. Yet it had a look of familiarity about it, that short row of shops just there, the brass plate on that house—yes, and round the corner, there was a park, and a big red brick building, a big house—— The car was moving slowly towards the drive. The front door opened. She was overwhelmed with dread. People were coming to welcome her, the nurse with the hard eyes, the doctor who always made her feel she was being punished, the matron with her false smiles—there, in their white coats and uniforms, smiling still, with big teeth like alligators—reaching out to her——

She screamed, and opened her eyes. Nicholas had stopped the car, and was looking at her with loving concern.

'Tansy? Are you all right?'

Tansy struggled to sit upright. Her skin was damp with sweat.

'A dream, that's all. A nasty dream.'

'Tell me about it,' he said quietly.

'I can't. You wouldn't understand.'

'Try me.'

'No—it was too confusing. I don't understand it myself.' Of course she understood it. It was the past coming to claim her, telling her she'd never be rid of it.

'All right now?'

'I'm fine.' They went inside the house, and Nicholas hung her jacket in the cloakroom.

'Why don't you lie down for a while?' he suggested. 'You look quite exhausted.'

'I couldn't impose like that. I'm fine, really.'

'Nonsense. This is doctor's orders. You go and lie down, and freshen up if you want to, the bathroom's en suite. I'll go and get the meal ready. Go on. My room's opposite Gemma's.'

When Tansy still hesitated, he came towards her, and tilted her chin.

'Aren't you sleeping well these days?' he asked, looking professional.

'Not really.'

'Something on your mind?'

'Something like that.' He seemed about to say something else, then changed his mind.

'Half an hour.' He guided her gently towards the stairs. Feeling like a bride on her wedding night, Tansy tiptoed across the landing, afraid to wake Gemma. She quietly opened the door he'd suggested, and entered a large room, seemingly full of sunshine. But the sun was starting to go down, and the sunny effect was due to the lovely imaginative mix of yellows and peaches and pinks in the room. She stood for a moment, taking it all in, the misty yellow curtains, the pale peach carpet, the Pre-Raphaelite print on the wall—was it a print, or the real thing? It looked like a Holman Hunt, but she was no expert. Her eyes rested on the pink and primrose duvet on the double bed, and she couldn't stop the flush that crept into her cheeks.

This was where he slept. This was where, if she wanted it, she could sleep, every night in his arms. Marry him, a little voice whispered. But I'd have to tell him the truth! She pulled off her shoes and skirt, and slipped under the duvet. Her last thought before she drifted away was the idea of waking every morning to see the sun streaming in, and hear the birdsong outside in the trees. She slept. At some point in her rambling dreams, she heard a door open, and something touched her forehead, like a soft feather.

When she woke she wasn't sure at first where she was. Then she heard the murmuring of voices downstairs, the chime of a clock, and kitchen noises at a distance. She jumped out of bed. How long had she slept? Had they been afraid to wake her? Oh, golly, she must have ruined their evening! Then she relaxed, as she caught sight of the little brass carriage clock on the bedside table. Seven-fifty. Just half an hour. And already she felt fresher.

She splashed water on her face, in the mimosa-yellow bathroom, and tidied up her hair. The faint shadows under her eyes seemed to have faded. She went back to the room for her bag. A photograph on the bedside table caught her eye, and she picked it up. It showed Nicholas—a much younger Nicholas, in shorts and T-shirt, on a beach somewhere. He had his arm around June, who looked much prettier there than in the later photograph. Her hair was short, her round face prettily plump, but not bloated and puffy. She looked plumper altogether, especially around her front. . . Had this been taken when she was pregnant with Gemma? She looked happy. Could all her problems have stemmed from the birth? Guilt?

Tansy quickly put down the photograph and left the room. She felt she had been intruding. As she reached the foot of the stairs, Nicholas appeared, a striped apron across his middle, his hair tousled. He had changed into casual trousers and a short-sleeved shirt.

'Dinner is ready, Your Ladyship,' he announced. 'You timed that well.'

'You forget we both worked as housemen on call in days gone by,' she reminded him.

'I shall never forget it! Come on, in here. Sit down. Did you sleep? You look better.'

'I did, thank you. I think I needed it.'

He had brought her into the kitchen. There was no sign of Beth. So who had he been talking to? Or could it have been a radio? Tansy settled herself down for the meal. And it was as delicious as the first time. And it occurred to Tansy that she really ought to return the compliment. But her flat was rather small. And intimate. She started on her grapefruit.

To follow, there was succulent duck with orange, and a selection of vegetables. They finished with coconut meringue, decorated with nuts and cherries. This concoction, Nicholas confessed, had come from the freezer!

'Was Beth here earlier?' asked Tansy, during the meal.

'She had to leave for a counselling session. A family that's just discovered they have HC.'

For a moment Tansy didn't reply. She chewed on a cherry. Then she said casually, 'I'm surprised Beth didn't tell you about the HC when you were engaged to her.'

His face seemed to close in. He stared at his plate and picked at a flake of meringue.

'That was why she went to America. She couldn't face telling me.'

'So that was why she was so angry with June! Of course, she didn't expect her sister to marry either. Why couldn't they have told you the truth at the outset?'

Nicholas shrugged. 'We all like to keep some little secrets, don't we? And some secrets are bigger than others, and some only seem immense. But they all have great importance to someone. I'm sure you understand.'

He spoke lightly, but the expression in his eyes was deadly serious.

'I can only agree with you, Nicholas,' Tansy said.

He reached across the table and took her hand.

'I've told you our most important secret, Tansy. Don't you have any you'd like to share?'

'They wouldn't be secrets then.'

'I don't want you to have secrets from me, Tansy. I want you to be able to tell me everything. I want you to trust me.'

She pulled her hand away. 'I don't know what makes you think I have a dreadful secret, Nicholas. If I do, it's not on the scale of yours, so it's not worth telling. I'm sorry.'

He frowned. 'How can we get married if you feel like that?'

'When did I say I was going to get married? Nicholas, I like you a lot, and I'm very fond of Gemma. But that's as far as it goes.'

The lies seemed to weigh heavily inside her, like a boulder.

'I'll get your coffee.' The silence seemed almost to be

solid as he poured the drinks and brought them to the table.

'Why are you so afraid to tell me about Rod?' he asked suddenly.

Startled, she looked up and the cup she had raised to her mouth shook in her fingers, and hot coffee spilled on to her hand. She jumped, dropping the cup, thrust her fingers in her mouth, and the tears spilled out, erupted like a volcano. Nicholas pulled her to him, murmuring and soothing her, until her sobbing had ceased. She tried to withdraw, but his embrace was strong.

'I'm all right—the coffee was hot, that's all——'

Nicholas sat her in the chair and examined the disaster area. There didn't appear to be much damage. He sat facing her.

'Why are you punishing yourself so much, Tansy?' he said quietly.

'Punishing?' she echoed.

'You know you only spilled the coffee because I mentioned Rod.'

'It was a shock. I didn't expect it. Did—Beth tell you?'

He nodded. 'I really didn't intend to shock you like that, but I could see something was tearing you apart, ruining your life. Ruining my life too, Tansy, because your happiness is my happiness. Can't you see that?'

'I suppose Beth has told you it all,' she muttered.

'I don't know what you mean by all, Tansy. She told me she'd met your mother in Carolina—Connie, is that right? And she told me you'd denied it, for some reason. Are you ashamed of your mother?'

'She talks too much,' muttered Tansy.

'I see. Yes, I think I do see what you mean. Well, Beth liked Connie—both outspoken, perhaps. They kept up a correspondence for a while. And Connie told her she had a daughter called Tansy, a doctor in Winchester.'

'This is Swindon.'

'But I told Beth you'd moved from Winchester. I couldn't see it was a crime. Beth told me you'd once known a doctor called Rod, and he'd died. And that's about all I know. Is there more?'

Tansy shook her head, afraid to meet his eyes in case he saw the truth.

'I was a student; he was a houseman. We were engaged—well, about to get engaged. Then he got killed. That's all.'

'How long ago was this?' Nicholas asked quietly.

'Six—seven years.'

'But, Tansy, you can't still be carrying your grief around like that! You're a psychiatrist, you should know it's not normal. All right, he meant the world to you, but he's dead, and you're alive, and there's a big world out here, full of living people, loving people. Why can't you love again?'

She felt a surge of relief. He didn't know it all.

'It wasn't as simple as all that, Nicholas. I loved Rod, probably too much. I gave him—everything.' She couldn't meet his gaze. 'And he betrayed my trust in him. He lied to me. When he crashed the car, he was on a road going somewhere else, with a girl I'd never heard of—Christina Swallow.'

Nicholas gasped. 'Swallow? The clinic in Andover?'

'He was giving up his ideas of being a neuro-surgeon, to pander to the wealthy hypochondriacs. If he'd lived, how could I ever have trusted him again?' Tansy's eyes were dark with remembered grief.

'Did Christina Swallow tell you this?' he asked.

'I've never met her. But it was obvious. I put two and two together.'

'And came up with five. Tansy, if I were to tell you Christina——'

'I don't want to know, Nicholas. It's over, forgotten.'

'But it isn't, Tansy. And if it isn't that that's spoiling everything between us, then there must be something else.'

'No, Nicholas. That's it—my secret. I'm sorry, but it won't change things between us. But now you know it all.'

And behind her back Tansy carefully crossed her fingers.

Tansy sat in an easy chair and watched Debbie Ross as she made clay models of her family. She had made her father first, appropriately in a dull grey colour, a thin figure with a hat and rather large feet. Then had come her mother, a large, lumpy figure in red clay—threatening? thought Tansy—with a huge bosom and high-heeled shoes. Now she was making herself, in nondescript brown. As she worked they talked.

'Tell me about your school friends, Debbie,' Tansy invited.

'Well, there's Natalie, she lives just round the corner, and Susan and Laura, and Carol, and Diane, and Zoe.'

'You do have a lot of friends!'

Debbie pulled off an arm and remodelled it. She glanced at Tansy. 'Not really. They're just in my class at school.'

'Who is your best friend? Natalie?'

'She was. But my mother wouldn't let me go to her house to play, and when she came to ours she wasn't allowed to play the games she wanted to, so she stopped coming. Then Laura started in our class, and now she's her best friend.'

'You don't have a best friend?'

'Not really. It doesn't matter. They only laugh at me. They laugh at my clothes, and my mother——' Debbie put the completed figure on the table and got up. 'I feel sick, Dr Tansy.'

'No, Debbie, I don't think you do,' said Tansy gently.

'I really do. May I go to the toilet?'

'There's a washbasin here, Debbie, if you really feel sick.'

'Will you leave the room?'

'No, I will not. I've seen lots of people being sick, Debbie. It doesn't bother me.'

Debbie was looking desperate. She cast urgent glances at the sink, then the door, then the sink again. She made a gagging noise in her throat. But Tansy remained unmoved.

'Please, Dr Tansy——'

'Weren't you sick this morning, Debbie?'

Debbie shook her head violently. 'I was nearly late for school.'

'No time to be sick, eh?'

'I—I didn't feel sick then.' Debbie cast an agonised glance at Tansy. 'But I really feel sick now.'

'Then go ahead. Use the washbasin.'

Reluctantly, Debbie crossed to the sink and stood over it, making retching noises. Her hand, as if it had a will of its own, fluttered up to her mouth, then dropped. When she turned back to Tansy, she was crying silently. Tansy got up.

'Come and sit by me, Debbie, and tell me all about it.'

At twenty past four Beth brought Gemma. Through her office window, Tansy had been aware of the heavy rain, and was not relishing the drive home, or even the dash across the wet car park. She'd been a fool to come in strappy sandals and a light dress, but the sun had been shining at half-past seven, and it had seemed warm and springlike. And what did it matter when one had a car?

She ushered out Mr Robbins and his autistic son, Liam. At the door Mr Robbins smiled his thanks, and took the appointment card. Four-year-old Liam, a beautiful child with blond hair and big blue eyes, reached out and took the card and solemnly smelled it before rubbing it over his face. When his father attempted to take it back the child screamed, a piercing shriek that must have sounded throughout the building.

Mr Robbins shrugged his shoulders. 'Good job I can remember it,' he said ruefully, and turned left outside the door.

'That's not the way out,' Tansy called.

'I know, Doctor, but Liam insists we always go this

way home, and you know what will happen if I try to change it.'

Tansy nodded. 'Another screaming session.'

She watched them as they walked down towards the psychology unit. The long way round. And when she turned to look in the opposite direction, she saw Beth through the waiting-room door. Not Gemma, because the window was high up. Beth was talking to someone, and laughing, and occasionally she glanced down, obviously at Gemma. She looked through the glass panels and saw Tansy. Tansy pushed the door open.

'Ready?' she asked Gemma. The child skipped towards her happily. She was wearing a yellow cotton jogging suit and a gold butterfly slide in her black curly hair. Beth, as usual, looked immaculate, this time in an emerald-green jumpsuit. She gave Tansy a smile.

'Sorry I can't stay. Nicholas asked me to give you this.' She took a folded piece of paper from her bag. Tansy accepted it, glancing at the heading.

'Oh, yes, the basic data form. Makes things a bit easier for me.'

She put it on top of the notes in her hand, and closed the file.

'Nicholas will be collecting Gemma,' said Beth. 'See you around.'

Gemma went straight across to the easel. 'I want to paint today, Dr Tansy. May I?'

'All right. But if I agree, will you paint what I ask you?'

Gemma pouted. 'Can't I paint a cat, then? I was going to paint a cat.'

'I've got a better idea,' said Tansy. 'You paint your house, and all your family in the garden. And a cat too, if you like.'

'We have a nice garden,' said Gemma, snatching up the brush. Tansy obligingly filled the jar with water.

'Are you painting, Dr Tansy? Daddy said you paint like a seven-year-old!' Gemma giggled.

'Oh, he did, did he? Can he paint any better, I wonder?'

'He does a lot of painting,' Gemma told her. 'He does seaside pictures, but no people on them. Cliffs and sea and things. I think I might like to be an artist when I grow up. I like painting animals.'

'Well, I shall watch you today,' said Tansy, as memories began to crowd in on her. 'And you can tell me all about the people as you paint.'

Gemma screwed up her nose and carefully drew the outline of the house. She was quite good for six, thought Tansy. Did she take after her father? It would be nice to be artistically gifted. Like Nicholas, by the sound of things. And Rod. Rod had painted horses. Laughingly, he had compared himself with George Stubbs. He had laughed a lot. He had made her laugh.

She felt the hot tears threaten, and turned her attention to what Gemma was doing.

The house was soon finished, with flowers and trees, and a strange-looking man with a wheelbarrow—a recognisable wheelbarrow.

'That's Fred, he's the gardener,' explained Gemma. 'He comes on Mondays for the heavy work. So this is a Monday.'

The figures slowly appeared: a woman with grey hair who was Mrs Coates, the daily help; Nicholas, in blue jumper and brown trousers, grinning with teeth like a crocodile; Beth, incredibly thin in yellow, but not smiling; June, sitting on a chair, an ugly creature with crooked legs and big sad eyes. Then Gemma herself, lots of teeth again, dressed in red. And a cat chasing a butterfly. Imaginative.

'And that's She,' said Gemma, finishing with a tall thin woman in a black dress, with long brown hair and glasses.

'She?' queried Tansy. 'A friend? Or a neighbour?'

'No. Just She. She won't come in, ever. She doesn't like me.'

'A teacher from school?' suggested Tansy, intrigued by this anonymous woman.

'No, no, no!' shouted Gemma, dabbing angrily at the picture with her brush, producing white blotches on the grass. 'She's—just—She! I've never seen her! She's horrible! She does awful things!'

Tansy sensed a crisis beginning. She went to her desk, and from a drawer produced a tube of Smarties.

'Would you like a sweet, Gemma? Do you like Smarties? Which colour do you like best?'

She held out the tube. But Gemma backed away, her eyes wide and frightened. She dropped the paintbrush, and stared in panic at the sweets.

'No—no—no! You'll kill me! You'll kill me! They'll take me into hospital, and I'll go all yellow! I shall tell Daddy! Daddy! I shall die!'

As she shrieked the words Gemma sidled around the room until she reached the door. And before Tansy could guess what was happening she ran out into the corridor, running as fast as her small legs would carry her.

'Gemma! Come back! What's wrong?' Heavens, how could Tansy have known a tube of innocent Smarties would set the child off like this?

Gemma had disappeared around the corner. The place seemed deserted. All Tansy could hear was the child's trainers as they slapped against the vinyl floor.

'Gemma! You haven't finished your painting!' As an incentive it didn't work. She started to follow, her sandalled feet tapping as she ran. Through the Psychology Department, round the corner and past the lifts. Gemma had run faster than Tansy had imagined. But she could still hear her footsteps, and they were quite a way ahead.

A door swung and banged shut. The footsteps seemed to stop. The stairs—she'd run down the stairs. And they led to the outside, the extensive grounds at the rear of the Outpatients Department. Trying not to imagine what an occurrence like this could do to her career, Tansy pulled open the swing door and started down the stairs. Far ahead, another door closed violently. Silence. Gemma was outside. And it was pouring with rain.

Tansy almost hurled herself through the ground-floor door. Ahead of her a path led to the left, round the building towards the front entrance. There was no sign of Gemma anywhere, and before her a dull leaden sky and a curtain of rain. Gemma was wearing just a thin cotton jogging suit. She'd be soaked—unless she was sheltering. Where could she shelter? To reach the nearest entrance she would have to follow the path to the front, and she'd still get very wet in the process. And would she risk coming back into the building when she felt she was at risk from Tansy?

'Gemma, you little fool!' whispered Tansy. 'Don't you know I love you, and I'd never do anything to hurt you?'

A terrible idea had occurred to her. If Gemma had run to the right, she would eventually come to the road, a busy road that was always full of traffic. And in her panic she could even run under——

Oh, God! prayed Tansy silently. Please let me find her! She started across the grass, deciding at the last moment to try the right-hand side of the building first. It posed the greater threat.

She'd never imagined this sort of thing could ever happen. Children did sometimes get very upset and frightened, but they invariably asked for their parents, waiting not far away. Nicholas could be anywhere in the hospital. Could Gemma have run to find him? In that case, wouldn't she have taken the path to the left, the most likely route? Was she wasting valuable time looking over here?

She was halfway to the road by now, and her thin cotton dress clung wetly to her skin, and flapped against her legs. Her feet were saturated from the wet grass.

'Gemma!' she called. 'Where are you? Gemma! I'll get your daddy for you!'

Why was there no one around to help? There were usually people crossing to the main hospital. Where were they all? And there seemed to be nowhere for Gemma to hide. She must have gone the other way!

Trying to stem her growing fear, she started to retrace her steps. Her chin-length golden hair slapped her face as she ran, her fringe stuck to her forehead.

'Gemma! Please come back, Gemma! Daddy will be waiting!' And what would Daddy say if he saw her like this? There was a soft sound as she rounded some bushes at the corner of the building. She paused.

'Gemma! Are you there?' Silence. Tansy skirted the dripping bushes carefully.

'Please, Gemma, you must come back. No one's going to hurt you. Gemma, we all love you!'

This time the sound was a definite sob, followed by a sniff. Frantically, Tansy wrenched the branches of the rhododendron bush apart, to reveal a very wet, very unhappy Gemma, squatting against the damp wall, rain running from her black curls down her face and neck. She didn't move as Tansy reached between the glistening dark green leaves.

'Come on, Gemma, you don't have to be upset. Come and tell me all about it. No one is going to be cross with you.'

'Not even if I killed her?'

'Killed who, Gemma?'

'My mummy. I killed her. I—I gave her my Smarties——'

As she spoke, in halting sentences, Tansy drew her out from her hiding-place and started to walk back with her to the rear entrance of the Outpatients building.

'Smarties aren't poisonous, Gemma,' she said gently.

'They couldn't have been real Smarties, then. Mummy told me never to take sweets from people. And she had some of my Smarties——' Gemma gulped.

'When was this, Gemma?'

'The day they took her away. And I heard them talking the next day. They said she'd taken something, tablets, and they'd killed her. But she didn't take them,

I gave them to her, and I couldn't tell Daddy, or Aunt Beth, because they cried, so they don't know!'

'Oh, Gemma!' Tansy drew the child to her as they reached the deserted Psychology Department. The child was so wet she was leaving drips of water behind her. Or was it herself? thought Tansy.

'And now I've told you, I supppose you'll tell Daddy and—— Will they send me away, Dr Tansy? Will I have to go to prison for years and years?'

Tansy squeezed her hand. 'Gemma, will you believe me when I say your Smarties didn't kill your mummy? She did take some tablets, real tablets, because she was ill, and she knew she wasn't going to get better, and she didn't want to upset you, lying there ill for a long time. She thought——' She swallowed hard. 'She thought you'd probably be happier with just your daddy and your Aunt Beth.'

It must have looked strange, Tansy thought afterwards, a doctor kneeling on the floor, dripping wet, holding an equally wet child to her, and both with tears mingling with the rain on their faces.

'I think Aunt Beth might go away,' said Gemma. 'I wish she would. Would you come and live with us then?'

'Oh, Gemma, that just isn't possible. And you mustn't say things like that about your aunt. She loves you very much.'

'Not as much as you. She doesn't hug me like Mummy did. It's because she's not my mummy. Only real mummies love their children.'

'Gemma, I'm not sure that's true,' said Tansy gently. 'I'm not your mummy, but you know I love you.'

The lump in her throat was so painful she could hardly swallow. She had always vowed she would never become emotionally involved with a patient, and now it had happened. Was it because Gemma was Nicholas's daughter? Or because she had to, because all her love that should have been given elsewhere had to go to someone?

She stood up. 'You're soaking wet, Gemma! I can't imagine what your daddy will say if he finds you like this. Come on, let's put you in some dry clothes and get you out of these wet ones.'

Silently, Gemma padded after her into her room. As Tansy started to remove the sodden jogging suit, Gemma said solemnly, 'I didn't kill Mummy, then?'

'Of course you didn't, darling! Mummy took your Smarties because she loved you.'

It was as though a dam had burst its banks. Sobbing, Gemma clung to her, and Tansy knew that this was the cure. And there'd be no need to see Gemma again. The answer had been so simple, but it had taken an unconscious gesture to reveal the truth. It had been a misunderstanding, as she'd thought. And she could tell Nicholas there should be no more problems arising from this situation. He would be very pleased that it had all been resolved so quickly.

She wiped Gemma's face, and pulled off the wet jogsuit top. 'Turn this way, pet,' she said, as she pulled off the cotton vest underneath. Gemma turned away to pick up the towel. She had her back to Tansy.

And, for a very long moment, Tansy felt quite faint. A pulse hammered in her head, she couldn't breathe.

Just below Gemma's left shoulder-blade was a red birthmark, in the shape of a bow, perfect even to the inch of ribbon hanging down. A bow of ribbon.

She swallowed. Her throat was so dry she could hardly speak. She touched the birthmark gently. Her voice was breaking as she said softly, 'Hello again, Rosalind.'

CHAPTER ELEVEN

'MY NAME isn't Rosalind,' said Gemma matter-of-factly. 'My second name is Rosemary. Had you forgotten?'

'Yes. Yes, I expect I had forgotten.' It was almost impossible to think coherently, let alone make sensible conversation. The one thing Tansy had often dreamed about, throughout the past six years, had finally happened. And without her even trying.

As she put Gemma's wet clothes on the radiator to dry, and found some undies and a cotton sweater and trousers in the cupboard, she was trying to convince herself it had to be a coincidence. Coincidences did happen—look at Beth meeting her mother halfway across the world. Was it Fate that caused her to be in the National Park that day, hundreds of miles away from Charlotte?

A little voice kept arguing that there were coincidences and coincidences. And whoever saw two identical birthmarks? An ordinary round one could easily be confused, but one shaped like a perfect bow of ribbon?

This is Rosalind, she said to herself, as she rubbed Gemma dry with the towel. As she held the child's body to her, she couldn't stop thinking, My Rosalind, my Rosalind.

It was only as she pulled the cotton sweater over Gemma's chest that an obvious weakness in her argument occurred to her. How could it be Rosalind? Hadn't June given birth to her? Hadn't Nicholas told her Gemma's birth had been normal? She bit her lip. She had been such a fool, such a fool. Jumping to conclusions again, just because some unfulfilled desire in her wanted to be met. Of course she had mistaken the birthmark, it was probably just similar to Rosalind's. Similar. Her eyes had seen what they wanted to see.

She had a sudden urge to pull up the child's sweater again, to have another look. But Gemma had gone across to the painting, and was looking at it critically. An idea came to Tansy.

'Gemma, tell me again about the lady in black. The one you call She.'

'She doesn't like me.'

'Have you ever met her? What's her name?'

'I've never seen her. Nobody's seen her. She doesn't have a name.' Gemma pulled the painting from the easel and screwed it up. Tansy was puzzled. Did Gemma have another problem that hadn't yet been resolved? Why did she hate She so much? Perhaps her therapy wasn't quite over.

'May I play with the dolls' house, Dr Tansy?' asked Gemma.

'Yes, of course. You play with the dolls' house while I do some work.'

She didn't really have any work, just the notes to write up. But she needed time to think. To think what she should do next. Nothing impulsive. How could she get absolute proof of her suspicion?

She glanced at Gemma, whose nose was screwed up as she concentrated. Tansy's heart began to sing again. Of course—Rod used to do that, she remembered now, quite vividly, as he painted his horses. He'd been very artistic. Had Gemma inherited his talent? Or Nicholas's? She sagged.

Here we go again, she chided herself, jumping to conclusions. Yet the more she looked at Gemma, the more she saw Rod. Rod had had black curly hair, but his eyes had been brown, not the deep pansy purple of Gemma's. She took a deep breath. Why hadn't she noticed it before? Gemma's eyes were almost the same colour as her own!

She is Rosalind! She must be!

What was I afraid of? she thought. Why did I give her up? Because I couldn't bear the thought that she'd look like Rod, and be a constant reminder of his betrayal?

She'd always thought it would be a boy. She was surprised when they told her. And shocked when they said she had to keep the baby with her until she left.

Rosalind—she had had to give her a name to be registered—hadn't looked like either of them. Small, born too early, she was like a doll. But not small enough to need special care. Six pounds two ounces.

Why hadn't she asked Nicholas her birth weight? What would she have thought if he'd said 'six pounds two ounces'? Coincidence? Probably.

She suddenly felt an exquisite pain, a need for him. The same feeling she had had after Rod had gone.

They had met at a New Year party at the hospital, a party arranged by some of the medical students, and held in the Hall of Residence. Tansy, at twenty, rather shy and naïve, had been roped in to join a game of Blind Man's Buff. With a university scarf over her eyes, her searching hands had eventually found a body which didn't twist out of the way when she tried to guess who it was. Her groping fingers had crept up a neck—suspiciously male—and then a smooth firm jaw—definitely male!—and lips had suddenly kissed her fingers. She squealed and pulled off the scarf, and looked into a fantastic pair of brown eyes. Their gazes locked, he grabbed her and kissed her, and there was a cheer from the other students.

'Come on, Rod, leave her alone! You've got to share her. Let somebody else have a chance! Let her catch somebody else!'

'Too late!' he laughed. 'She's mine!'

From then on their lives revolved around each other. Laughing, joking—Rod was always laughing—looking into each other's eyes, holding hands.

How could he have deceived her? thought Tansy, watching Gemma as she moved furniture in the dolls' house. Hadn't he constantly told her he loved her? All she knew was she had never been happier. One day they would be together for ever, of that she was certain.

She took him home to meet her mother, who jokingly

remarked she should have been twenty years younger! Rod had even seemed to get on with Ted, Connie's brash American friend.

The months had sailed by on clouds of happiness. Then Connie announced their wedding: July the twenty-seventh. Tansy, being a second-year medical student, was on vacation, and Rod had succeeded in getting a few days' holiday too, before starting a resident house job in Reading. As usual, Connie had invited everyone she could think of, and then there were Ted's relatives and friends from Carolina.

After the short register office wedding, with Connie dressed in bright yellow, and Ted in white—which didn't suit him—the Wiltshire country house was soon full of noisy, laughing guests. Tansy hardly noticed, because Rod was there, and she wondered if he was thinking what she was. Would the next wedding be theirs?

Connie and Ted left for the airport and a honeymoon in Venice. Connie had left Tansy to organise the sleeping arrangements for the three guests who were staying the night—two of Ted's cousins from Carolina, and Rod. The other American guests were staying in hotels, making the most of their visit to England.

The two elderly cousins, extremely tired after their journey and the bustle of the wedding and reception, retired to bed early. Rod looked at Tansy and she knew what he wanted. It was like a magnetic force that drew her into his arms. His kiss was passionate, his touch like fire. She tried to resist, but it was like a drug; she felt she'd been hypnotised.

They sank on to the thick rug in front of the fire, Rod's hands eager, his mouth demanding. And all she wanted to do was give. She made a token gesture of protest, but what was the point in protesting, when this was what she had been waiting for for so long, this pure ecstasy?

*   *   *

On August the third, Rod had to leave. 'I start my new job tomorrow,' he had explained.

'Sunday?' queried Tansy.

'That's what they said.'

She believed him. And she didn't want him to go. The past week had been heaven, and it had passed far too quickly. But he had to go. He kissed her and threw his case into the back of his red sports car. She straightened the collar of his emerald-green shirt.

'Drive carefully,' she pleaded. 'I love you! Ring me this evening.'

'Sure thing. Love you!'

'Love you!'

The car roared away, and Tansy went back to the empty house. Tomorrow Connie and Ted would return.

It was six o'clock when the doorbell rang. Mystified, chewing on a ham sandwich, she went to answer it.

'Miss Tansy Blair?' The policeman was young and serious. The policewoman was plump and red-haired. They sat on the sofa, and she heard their words through a haze. She must have fallen asleep on the sofa, this had to be a dream. No, a nightmare. She spoke through dry lips.

'Dead?'

'Instantly. He didn't suffer.'

Tansy felt anger welling up in her. Here this policeman was, telling her her world had fallen apart, and all he could say was 'He didn't suffer.' As if that made it all right!

'Where?' She croaked the words. 'Where did it happen?'

The policeman consulted his notebook. 'On the A342 not far from Andover.'

'A place called Ludgershall,' added the policewoman.

'No, that can't be right,' argued Tansy. 'You must mean the A4 to Reading. Is it Newbury you mean? He would have gone through Newbury.'

'It appears he was going to Andover,' repeated the

policeman patiently. 'We haven't yet been able to question his passenger, a young lady. She was still unconscious when we left.'

Tansy put her hands to her head. She didn't understand a word of this.

'I must be going mad! He was going—alone—to work in Reading! He couldn't be on the road to Andover with a girl!' The police officers exchanged glances which she didn't miss. 'You've made a mistake! It's someone else! We were going to get married——'

She buried her face in her hands.

'If it's any help,' said the policeman impassively, 'the girl in the car is nineteen and her name is Christina Swallow. She's very badly hurt. Head injuries.'

'Never heard of her,' muttered Tansy.

'Her father owns a large private clinic in Andover—Swallow Court. Very expensive, so I believe.'

Tansy couldn't answer.

Connie and Ted did their best to comfort Tansy, but they were full of their own plans to move to Carolina. And Connie had never quite realised how serious Tansy had been about Rod. She was excited, buying lots of new clothes, and Tansy felt her mother would hardly miss her when she went back to university.

She still felt numb inside. The only name that repetitively surfaced was Christina Swallow. Why hadn't Rod ever mentioned her? What was she, some wealthy socialite? Could he have been contemplating a future as a private doctor in a clinic that catered for rich hypochondriacs? He had been so determined to specialise in neurosurgery. A brain surgeon. She thought he had meant it.

She tried to get absorbed in her studies, tried to forget. But, as the days went by, and she made an effort to get involved in university life again, another worry surfaced. She had put it down to shock at first, but after three months was that likely? Only one thing to do. Go and see someone.

The pregnancy test was positive. Tansy didn't know

who to confide in. Connie and Ted had been in Carolina
for a month. No help in that quarter. And abortion was
distasteful to her. She was training to save life, not
destroy it.

Connie had sold the Marlborough house, and settled
twenty thousand pounds in Tansy's bank account. Tansy
was afraid to touch it. But it might come in handy for
the weeks around the baby's birth, and afterwards.

Connie's next letter, after Tansy had told her the
news, was full of advice, but none of it practical. Connie
wished she were still in England to look after the baby
when it arrived. But Ted wasn't fond of England. So
why couldn't Tansy go and live with them in the States?

Out of the question, thought Tansy. I'm going to be a
doctor, remember? And I've got two and a half years to
go. Connie's next suggestion was to keep the baby, and
once it was at school to go back to medical school and
finish the course.

No chance, thought Tansy. I probably wouldn't get
back in, a mature student of twenty-six, and an
unmarried mother at that.

She was fortunate that her pregnancy caused no health
problems, no morning sickness, no indigestion, no
muscle cramps. When she finally revealed her secret to
her friends, she was surprised by their attitude. There
was no moralising, no accusations, just sympathy at
losing Rod and now having to face this. One of her
closest friends, Mary, became quite excited as the weeks
went by. One day she came back from a shopping trip
with a pair of white knitted bootees. Tansy stared at
them, and tears came to her eyes.

'No, Mary, I'm sorry. I've been thinking this thing
through, and I've made up my mind. I'm having the
baby adopted.'

'Tansy, you can't! It's Rod's baby, something to
remember him by.'

Tansy shook her head. She had told no one that Rod
had betrayed her, told lies, and had obviously been
making plans for the future that didn't include herself.

'I shall never forget Rod, whatever happens,' she said sadly. 'But I don't need to carry my grief around with me. It will be better for the baby, better for me. I shall be able to carry on with my life, my career. Who knows?' And she gave a little laugh. 'Perhaps I wasn't cut out for marriage and a family, and I'm sure I wouldn't have been happy doing part-time medicine!'

Who was she trying to fool? she thought later. Herself?

She spent Christmas at Mary's parents' house in Leicester. She didn't have a home base any more, and had no intention of putting down roots yet, and buying a house. Mr and Mrs Barlow were extremely considerate and understanding, and once she almost suspected they might offer to look after the baby themselves!

Then spring came, and Tansy began to feel tired, her body unwieldy. March crept into April, and on April the sixth—two weeks before the baby was due—Tansy admitted herself into the small private maternity unit on the outskirts of Southampton. She hadn't wanted to be among other satisfied mothers, on one big ward, knowing that she alone would be going home without a baby.

She was given a small single room which overlooked the park, with dark green curtains and a picture of windmills on the plain cream wall opposite the bed. It was then she wished she had Rod with her, but she'd have to make do with Mary to hold her hand and encourage her through her hours of labour.

The baby was born at three o'clock in the morning of April the seventh, a tiny red creature with fuzzy dark hair and long eyelashes. Tansy was afraid to look. She expected them to take her away and put her in the nursery. They must have known she was having her adopted.

'I'm afraid you'll have to keep her with you until you go home,' the midwife said in her brisk way. 'It's the rules. But we've informed your social worker, and she'll come for the baby on the day you're due to go home.'

Tansy stared at her in amazement. Was this some sort

of punishment for having a baby out of wedlock? It wouldn't have been born out of wedlock if Rod hadn't died. They'd have married. Or would they? Had she been duped, like lots of other girls?

'But that's cruel!' she protested. 'How can I look after her for three days, and grow to love her, then just let her go?'

'It's your decision, dear.'

The other midwife was firm but not unkind. She gave her the baby to hold, and Tansy knew straight away that this would be the hardest thing she had ever done in her life. Could she do it?

The baby was perfect, she thought, as she changed her nappy and stroked her soft skin. On the second day the midwife was watching her as she changed the baby's nightie. She lay over her knees, and Tansy stared in amazement.

'Oh,' she said. 'She's got a birthmark.'

'Yes, but it will probably fade,' said the midwife.

'It's like—a bow of ribbon,' said Tansy wonderingly.

On the third night—a Wednesday—Tansy didn't sleep. She didn't want nine o'clock to come, when the social worker would arrive. During Wednesday night she stood in her pyjamas at the square window and pulled back the green curtains. Outside it wasn't as dark as she'd expected. Black trees bent in the wind. An owl flew silently overhead. There was no stars. The moon was half hidden by a cloud. Windy, she thought. Rain tomorrow. And she prayed for help to cope with what she was going to do.

Next morning she fed the baby, and dressed her in a pink babygro she had bought specially. As she talked to her in low tones she was sure the baby was watching her. Such beautiful navy-blue eyes. Such eyelashes!

'I wanted to keep you, remember that, Rosalind. I love you more than anyone in the whole world. But I'm doing it for you. This way you'll have all the opportunities I can't give you on my own.'

She held the baby to her breast and kissed the downy pink cheek. The baby made a cooing noise. Quickly Tansy laid her in the perspex cot, and covered her with a blanket. She just wanted it to be over.

At half-past nine she was standing at the window again, watching the children in the park. For half an hour she had entertained vain hopes that the social worker wouldn't come, no one would come, Rosalind would be hers. Foolish, adolescent ideas.

The children in the park were too young for school. The mothers stood talking, snatching a few leisure moments before going home to do the cleaning, or going shopping for food. Such ordinary, placid lives. The sky was darkening.

Behind her, she heard the door open. She was afraid to turn round.

'I've come, Tansy.' The social worker was a small, dark woman with an understanding smile.

'Yes,' said Tansy.

'Is she ready?'

'Yes.'

There were sounds of movement behind her. The baby gave a little cry and Tansy clenched her fists to stop herself from turning round and saying, 'No, you can't have her! I've changed my mind!'

She held her breath. Soft footsteps crossed to the door.

'I'm going, Tansy. Are you sure you don't——'

'No. Please go.'

'I'll be in touch. Goodbye, Tansy.' The door opened and closed. And when Tansy turned round, the cot was empty. And the rain beat against the window.

Tansy wiped her eyes. Remembering that day always upset her. Gemma had taken all the dolls out of the house, and had arranged them for a picnic, seated around a table.

'Do you want tea, Mummy?' she was asking the June doll, and poured water from a toy teapot into a tiny cup.

A trained professional, Tansy found she was automatically analysing the situation. A Gemma doll seated next to the Nicholas doll. The June doll and the Beth doll together. Even the cat with a saucer of water, meant to be milk. But she didn't have a cat, thought Tansy. I never saw one. I'll have a word with Nicholas. A pet would help her.

At the corner of the house stood another figure. By accident? thought Tansy. A woman in dark blue. Not black? No—none of the female figures had been dressed in black. Was dark blue the nearest shade she could find? She. And the feeling was growing in Tansy that she knew who She was.

I have to know for sure, she said to herself, before I speak to Nicholas. She turned the pages of Gemma's file, to the top one. Gemma's date of birth: April the seventh. There was a roaring in her ears. She wanted to sing, she wanted to shout, I've found Rosalind! I've found my daughter!

And in the same heart-crushing instant she realised it was the last thing she could do. How could she possibly tell Nicholas he had adopted her child? A feeling of cold dread suddenly enveloped her. Did Beth already know about the baby? Had her mother told her? Oh, God, did Nicholas know she'd had a child, given it away? And she was a child psychiatrist, who professed to love children, who tried to straighten out their confused lives. She hadn't been able to face up to her own problem. She'd been a coward, had turned her back on it. That was what he would think.

The clock showed five-thirty. Gemma's clothes were nearly dry. Tansy moved them around on the radiator. There came a sharp rap at the door. She swallowed. Her mouth was dry.

'Come in,' she called.

Nicholas looked tired and haggard. She wanted to take him in her arms and kiss the weary lines away, but she restrained herself.

'Sorry I'm rather late. Is she ready?'

'Yes. Has something happened?'

'One of my patients just died. They don't all survive, you know, just because they're children.' He spoke angrily.

'I know, Nicholas. I know.'

He seemed to notice her for the first time, and he came towards her. For an agonising moment she was sure he was going to take her in his arms and kiss her. Then his glazed eyes seemed to clear.

'How is she?' he asked.

It was the love in his voice and his eyes that did it. Despite her earlier intentions of acting logically, she spoke impulsively. She said painfully, 'Nicholas, why didn't you tell me Gemma was adopted?'

There was a long pause. She held her breath. His eyes were searching her face. He frowned.

'I'm right, aren't I? She was adopted?'

Slowly he nodded. 'Yes, Tansy, she was.'

CHAPTER TWELVE

ALL Tansy could hear was her own heart beating, and the heavy rain at the windows. A rainy day when I lost her, she thought. A rainy day when I found her. She forced herself to look at Nicholas, to keep calm.

'Why didn't you tell me? Or did you think it was irrelevant, like June's suicide, and the Huntington's Chorea?'

He sank into a chair as if all the fight had been knocked out of him.

'No, it isn't irrelevant. I suppose it must be very important, at least to Gemma. And I didn't tell you because I was sure Gemma would. She must have told you about the woman she calls She? Yes, of course she has, or you wouldn't be asking me about it now.'

Tansy caught her breath. She hadn't thought this out at all well. How could she have known about the adoption if Gemma hadn't told her? Knowing any other way could only implicate her. The birthmark wasn't supposed to have told her anything. She recalled how uncertain she must have sounded when she'd asked Nicholas to confirm her suspicion. If Gemma had told her she would have been sure. Had he noticed?

She nodded. 'That's right—Gemma told me about She.' Which was quite true. 'But I'd rather you'd told me at the outset. It confused me a great deal.'

'I can assure you Gemma has no hang-ups about it. We told her all about it when she was four, and asking questions about everything. She seemed to understand it very well. She never talks about it now.'

Tansy didn't answer. She glanced across at the child, who was busy putting the dolls to bed. She watched as Gemma picked up the She doll and put it in a room of its own. Could that mean Gemma hadn't completely written off the woman who had given birth to her? Tansy felt a surge of maternal love for the child. Then a thought occurred to her.

'Nicholas, you said you didn't know about the HC until June began to feel ill. But surely that was why you adopted Gemma? Because of the genetic risk?'

He shook his head. 'No, it wasn't like that. I, naturally, wanted children, but they didn't arrive. So June went for some tests. And she couldn't have any.' He stared at Tansy, and a look of dawning realisation came over his face. 'I should have thought there was something wrong then. She didn't seem to be at all unhappy about it. She was only too eager to adopt. I didn't suspect anything. I just thought she was being very mature about it. I remember thinking, when I found out about the HC, how fortunate it was we didn't have any natural children.'

It sounded genuine. He had to be telling the truth. Tansy nodded.

'It's understandable.'

Nicholas glanced at Gemma. 'Have you managed to sort anything out yet?'

'I think so. She did have a misunderstanding about a few things she'd overheard. I hope I've managed to straighten them out for her.'

'You must feel proud of yourself.'

'I'm more relieved than proud,' said Tansy. 'Relieved that she can't get Huntington's Chorea.'

'Unless her real parents——'

'No, they don't——' She had spoken without thinking. Nicholas was watching her intently. She flushed.

'That would be too much of a coincidence, wouldn't it?'

He nodded. 'You must think me an absolutely deplorable patient's parent! So many things I assumed you knew, so many things I felt you didn't need to know. You must forgive me. And, honestly, I'm sure there isn't anything else I've missed out!'

'I hope there isn't!'

'I should have told you about the adoption earlier, but, to be honest, I tend to forget Gemma isn't our natural daughter.' Nicholas cast the child a loving, paternal glance, and Tansy felt an unaccountable twinge of jealousy.

'Her mother must have been a beautiful girl,' Nicholas added. 'She was only twenty-one when Gemma was born—they told us that much. It was a private adoption, you see, so we learned a bit more than usual.'

Tansy felt a band constricting her chest. How much had he been told?'

'Is that a good thing?' she found herself saying.

'You mean in the future, if Gemma ever tries to find her mother? Surely it will be easier for her?'

'The mother may not want to be found.' She was mouthing platitudes. Of course she'd want to be found! This was Gemma they were talking about!

Nicholas shrugged. 'A possibility. But a great pity, because I'd like to meet her. I shall always be in her debt. Gemma's been one of the best things to happen to me.'

Gemma had put away the dolls and had overheard her name. She scrambled to her feet.

'What does that mean, Daddy? I was the best thing for what?'

Nicholas hugged her. 'It just means I love you more than almost anyone else in the whole world.' Almost, thought Tansy. For an instant his eyes met hers, and she was embarrassed by the emotion in them. If only she could tell him the truth! And her throat hurt with unshed tears.

'So Gemma doesn't need to see you again?' he asked.

'I think once more, to tie up the loose ends, you might say. She's a very bright child. But she's only six, and she's likely to misunderstand things the adults say.'

He nodded. His grey eyes searched her face.

'Yes, she is bright. Her mother was a university student.'

'Really?' Why was he looking at her like that? He

couldn't possibly know her baby was Gemma. He couldn't even know she'd had a baby—unless Beth knew. How much *had* Connie told her?

'When do you want to see her?' Nicholas asked.

Relieved at the detached tone in his voice, she flicked the pages of her appointments book. Thursday. She'd squeezed in Désirée at twelve-thirty. That would shorten her lunch hour. Sarah Crosby was coming after school at four o'clock. Debbie—oh, she was during the morning. She looked up.

'Is quarter to two awkward for you?' she asked. 'It's earlier than I usually start, but I can give her half an hour then. Unless you'd rather wait until next week, Tuesday——' She turned the pages.

'Quarter to two is fine. Beth should be free.' As he rose his gaze rested on the yellow jogging suit on the radiator. Tansy followed his glance.

'She went outside in the rain,' she explained. 'She was a little upset—my fault, I'm afraid. And I didn't realise it was raining so hard. But they should be dry now. You can bring back the other clothes some other time.'

She folded up the dry clothes and handed them to him. Their fingers touched, and a tingle ran through her body. Their eyes met, his expression enigmatic. Then he turned away and walked to the door.

'Coming, Gemma?'

Tansy's gaze fixed on the child hungrily as she ran to Nicholas and took his hand. Her every instinct wanted her to beg her to stay.

'See you on Thursday, Gemma.' She tried to smile, and stifled the urge to run and hold her tightly.

'I'll slip in some time,' said Nicholas. 'We can talk about all this. What about the dining-room tomorrow?'

Her mouth dry, she answered, 'Sure. About one?'

The door closed behind a waving Gemma, and Tansy heard her skipping footsteps along the deserted corridor. She slumped in her chair. Nicholas had seemed almost like a stranger. She sighed. She'd better start realising her troubles were all of her own making. Nicholas was

Gemma's father. Now she'd rejected him, would he turn again to Beth? Damn it, Tansy! You've turned down Nicholas, and you're never going to get your baby back!

She put her head on the desk and burst into deep, wrenching sobs.

Next day, Tansy felt as though someone had pulled the ground from beneath her feet. She went through all her ward routines automatically, and only remembered Nicholas's lunch arrangement when the ward phone rang at eleven-thirty with a message from his secretary. Dr Vernon had been called away to a meeting at the Memorial Hospital in Cirencester, and would be having lunch there. He'd make another arrangement with her.

Tansy put down the phone numbly. It didn't matter. Nothing mattered any more. She had a sudden urge to run away, leave the hospital, leave Swindon. Just leave and never come back. But she was still sane enough to realise that her sort of pain would only go with her wherever she went. Running away solved nothing.

She wrote out the forms for Gerald Macey's EEG, and rang the Scanner Unit to find out when he could go for a CAT-scan of his head.

Bonnie was now calling herself Emily, and asking about Mrs Walsh's dog, Rufus. She had no memory of anyone called Heather or Patty. It was going to be a long and difficult task, to merge the two personalities as one again.

The ward meeting that afternoon went smoothly, and Tansy responded mechanically to Dan's questions about the patients. She hoped it wouldn't go on too long. She wanted to get home. She'd been right all along. Relationships only brought pain. The meeting ended. She grabbed her papers and started to leave. At the door Dan called her name.

'Dr Blair!' Hattie was still talking to Ellen Chalmers. Tansy turned, smiling.

'Yes, Dr Rice?'

Dan pointedly waited until the others had gone.

'Are you all right, Tansy?' he asked.

'Yes, I'm fine.'

'You're very pale. You look ill. Sister told me you don't seem as lively as usual. She said you were a bit vague during the ward round. Is something wrong? Can I help?'

His soft voice threatened to break down her defences. She suddenly wished she could put her head on his shoulder and tell him everything. She bit her lip. Her throat hurt with the emotion.

'I've just got—something on my mind at the moment. Don't worry, it will clear. Just give me a couple of days.'

He put a hand on her shoulder. 'Would you like to have a couple of days off? I can take your patients.'

'No, that's not necessary. It will be better if I work— keep busy and all that.'

'If that's how you want it.'

Tansy flashed him a smile and hurried from the room, leaving him looking after her, his papers still scattered on the table.

The phone rang as she stepped out of the bath. Hugging a towel around her, she picked up the receiver.

'Tansy?'

She quivered at his voice. But she was still feeling hurt by the cancelled appointment, and she spoke curtly.

'Yes, Nicholas?'

'Sorry about lunch today—I just couldn't avoid it. And it was so boring, all about finance and management, and all the time I wanted to be with you——'

'Please, Nicholas, I wish——' she began.

'I wish too, Tansy, I wish you could trust me enough to love me——'

If only you knew how much I do! she cried to herself. 'You're making it very hard for me, Nicholas——' she began.

'You see? You want to love me, in fact, I know you already do. Why are you so afraid to tell me? Why are you punishing yourself like this?'

'Are you ringing to make another appointment for Gemma?'

'Gemma? Oh, yes, that's why I'm ringing, actually. She won't be able to come and see you tomorrow. She's not very well.'

'What's wrong?' She hoped he hadn't noticed the panic in her voice.

'Just a chill, I expect. She's a wee bit feverish—sore throat. You know what children are like: at death's door one day, perfectly well the next. You don't need to worry about her, Tansy.'

'No, of course not. But you will still call in to talk about her, won't you?'

'Do you want me to?'

'That's not the point. She's my patient, you're her father. You need to know what her problem was.' She spoke stiltedly.

'Why don't you come here to talk about it?' asked Nicholas. 'As it won't be a consultation with Gemma, our house must be just as adequate as the hospital. And more comfortable.' Inexplicably, she thought of his room, and the sunny double bed.

It was very tempting. But she'd have to be so careful not to give anything away. She'd have to be constantly on her guard. Could she do it, away from the professional atmosphere in her office, the desk between them? But she could see Gemma again.

'I'm very tempted,' she admitted. 'And it would be nice to be able to reassure myself that Gemma isn't at death's door!' She tried to joke about it.

'You're very fond of her.'

She drew her breath in sharply. 'Of course. Who couldn't be? And she's your daughter.'

'Tansy, what does that remark mean?'

'It means nothing, Nicholas. Just that I'll come to your house if you want me to. To talk about Gemma, nothing more.'

'Point taken.'

'Wednesday today. Do you mean this week? Or next?'

'It will have to be during the next couple of days,' said Nicholas. 'We're going away on Saturday.'

'Oh.' Words would have been inadequate to express what she felt. He was going away. Gemma was going away. Beth too, presumably. For long? She deliberately didn't ask, in case he thought it had affected her.

'Beth will be out tomorrow night,' he said slowly. 'Eight o'clock?'

'I'll be there.'

And as she went back to her bedroom to slip on a robe, she couldn't help feeling it was going to be a momentous occasion. But she wasn't sure how.

Debbie Ross sat on the floor making a Lego house. She was wearing school uniform, grey pleated skirt and navy sweatshirt. Her nondescript hair was tied in a plait at the nape of her neck. It didn't suit her, made her small pale face appear naked and unprotected, her big light blue eyes vulnerable.

'Which school do you go to, Debbie?' asked Tansy.

'Lainesmead Junior.'

'You finish there soon?'

'In July. I'm going to Churchfields in September.'

'Looking forward to it?'

Debbie shrugged. 'I don't know. I like Lainesmead.'

'Won't you feel grown-up once you're at a secondary school?'

'I don't know.' Debbie looked up at Tansy. 'Is it nice being grown-up, Dr Tansy?'

'Well, I like it,' said Tansy. Sometimes, at least. 'Think of all the things you'll be able to do that you can't do now. Isn't that exciting?'

'I suppose so. Do people have to get married, Dr Tansy? I mean, can't they just have careers?'

'I'm not married. I enjoy my career,' Tansy said solemnly.

'My mother keeps talking about when I'm grown-up and married and have got children of my own, but I don't think I want to get married. I think I'd like to be a teacher—a sports teacher.'

'You can be a teacher and still be married.'

It had become obvious to Tansy that Debbie had a lot of problems concerning her approaching puberty. For some reason growing up posed a threat. Yet at the same time she longed for autonomy, control over her life.

Mrs Ross had been a dominant influence for too long. Unconsciously, Debbie wanted to be rid of that authority, that control over her. By only keeping down certain foods, she felt she was exerting control over her growth, her body.

'Has your mother bought you the jeans yet, Debbie?' Tansy asked.

'Not yet. I thought I might ask Daddy.'

Tansy felt a little surge of hope. So Hattie had started to do her work. Mr Ross had emerged from the shadows.

'Do you think he will?' she asked.

'He said my pink dress was horrid. He's never said anything like that before. Mother was speechless!' Debbie laughed. It was the first time Tansy had seen her laugh. It was a lovely, hopeful sign.

'Tell me about the ballet classes, Debbie.'

'I'm giving them up. But I haven't told Mother yet. Because I want to join a football team.'

Just before lunch Désirée came bouncing in. There was a pink glow in her round, pale cheeks, and her eyes shone.

'Where's your mother, Désirée?' asked Tansy.

'I told her to wait out there. This is between you and me.'

Tansy was taken aback. 'That sounds ominous, Désirée,' she said, smiling at the fat, usually depressed fifteen-year-old. And what had the girl done to her mousy, stringy hair? It had been cut quite short, and waved prettily into her neck.

'You see Dr Tansy, I really want some advice. All the other girls I know seem to know things I don't.'

'That sounds mysterious, Désirée. Tell me more.'

Désirée leaned forward on the desk. 'Tell me, Dr
Tansy—I mean, you're very pretty, and you must have
lots of boyfriends, so you'll know what I mean.'

Boyfriends? A few days ago, Tansy would never have
made the connection with Désirée Lawrence.

'I'll help if I can,' she promised, feeling she was the
last person to give the girl advice. 'You've got a
boyfriend?'

'Well, no, not yet. I wasn't much bothered with boys.
But there's this boy just started in the fifth form. Oh,
he's dreamy, Dr Tansy! He looks ever so intelligent, and
he's got these big brown eyes, and he's tall—oh, Dr
Tansy, what can I do to make him notice me?'

'You've already made a start,' said Tansy. 'Your hair
looks very nice, and——' she recalled the girl's mother's
anxious words, and decided to act on a hunch '—I do
believe you're slimmer.'

Désirée jumped up and pirouetted on the carpet. 'Do
you really think so, Dr Tansy? I've been dieting, you
see, but I didn't tell Mom, she'd have been too shocked!
I cut out chocolate and chips and biscuits. Mom thinks
I'm off my food!' she laughed.

'I think you ought to tell her,' Tansy advised her.
'She's quite worried about you.'

'Will it take a long time to get really slim, Dr Tansy?
Because this boy—his name's Matthew—he seems keen
on Hayley Fenner, and she's like a model. Could I be a
model one day, do you think?'

Oh, dear, thought Tansy, this was really asking for
the moon. And don't we all do it? She leaned across the
desk.

'Désirée, I can't give you any better advice than to
make the most of yourself, but always be natural, be
yourself, not some false actress in the films. Everyone
has their good points. And being pretty isn't everything.
You're not ugly, Désirée. You have nice eyes—make the
most of them. And one day the right boy will come

along. It may not be Matthew, but he'll be the one for you. And you'll know it.'

'Do you think so? Oh, Dr Tansy, I feel so much better for coming to see you!'

'That's nice.' Ironic, thought Tansy. For months I've been trying to encourage her, boost her sagging self-esteem, and now falling in love has done it at one fell swoop. Yet she thanks me!

'Do I have to come and see you again?' Désirée was asking.

'Well, the way you are now, I'd usually say no. But I'm dying to know how this love affair works out, so come and see me in three months, and give me a progress report. All right?'

Tansy scribbled a date on Désirée's card.

'I'm so happy,' said Désirée.

'It's wonderful what love can do,' murmured Tansy.

She hurried back from lunch. She didn't feel like sitting and making polite conversation in the dining-room. She picked up Sarah Crosby's file from her desk and flicked through the pages. For once, she wished she could pass all these problems on to someone else. She was letting herself get involved.

But Gemma wasn't a patient. Not now. Yet hadn't she felt involved before her discovery? Had there been some instinctive bond between them, a bond that had never been truly broken six years ago?

Perhaps she was deluding herself. Yet for most of last night she had tossed and turned, tried to imagine the last six years if they'd been different, if she'd kept Gemma—Rosalind—for herself. It would have been almost impossible to devote herself to her medical training, while caring for a young child. But she would have watched her grow, heard her first words. Mummy. Her heart seemed to wrench apart.

She knew she was being sentimental, but she kept imagining herself walking along the street, the child's soft, trusting hand in hers, the admiring glances of strangers at the contrasting pair. Contrasting! That was it! That was what had seemed so strange in the tea-shop. Gemma didn't look like Nicholas, nor Beth, nor June. And now she knew why. Because she looked so much like Rod. Except for the eyes; she had her own violet eyes. But they couldn't be too much alike, or people would have commented on it. They'd have—— She stopped dead. Beth. Mending her sandal. She'd said something about her eyes, how similar. . . But that had been ages ago. And she still couldn't know about Gemma and herself. No one knew.

It was almost time for the first patient. The phone rang.

'Child Psychiatry. Dr Blair.'

'Tansy? It's Beth.'

'Is something wrong, Beth? Is it Gemma?'

'Well, yes, it is, actually, Oh, she isn't any worse. Is that what you thought? No, Nicholas is pretty confident she'll be all right for Scotland on Saturday.'

'That surprised me a bit, when he told me you were all going to Scotland.' Tansy tried to sound unconcerned, feeling she had already given too much away with her panicky reaction to the call.

'Did it? It was planned ages ago. Had to be, really. But Tansy, I rang to ask you if you'd seen a little green plastic frog, one of those Kermit things. You know?' said Beth.

'A frog?' queried Tansy.

'Gemma took it with her to the hospital. It's a sort of lucky mascot to her. She won't go to Scotland if its not found—you know what children are like. She said she had it in your room.'

Tansy thought back to yesterday. Such a lot had happened.

'I don't remember, Beth, but I may have put it away with the other toys. I'll look for it, and if I find it I'll bring it with me tonight.'

'Oh, good!' Beth cleared her throat. 'I've never

thanked you, Tansy, for helping Gemma. She means a lot to me, and she's so much happier now.'

'I'm very pleased. I hope you find Scotland agreeable.'

'But we know Scotland well. My mother lives there— Kilmarnock. And she does get very lonely at times. That's why we decided just a few days would be worse than useless.'

Tansy's mouth was dry. More than a few days. Weeks? 'So you're going to be away some time?' she queried.

'For good. Didn't Nicholas tell you? It's the only thing, really. The way things are.'

The way things are.

'I'm sure it's the best thing, Beth. You're quite right.' Tansy put down the phone. For good. For ever. The words seemed to echo inside her head. She put her face in her hands, forcing back the tears. A huge hollow lay inside her. Nicholas was leaving her, just when she was beginning to realise she couldn't live without him. And she had found Gemma, only to lose her almost at once. It would have been better if she'd never found her at all.

Sarah Crosby sat by the dolls' house, listlessly moving the dolls backwards and forwards. Tansy noticed the father doll was left alone in the corner.

'Were you disappointed about not getting to the Grammar School in Salisbury?' asked Tansy. Instinctively, she had felt this was at the root of the trouble.

'A bit.'

'Do you like your aunt?'

'She's all right.'

'Has she got a nice house?'

Sarah shrugged. She pushed a tiny bed into a corner.

'Have you stayed with her before?' asked Tansy.

'No.'

'But you were looking forward to staying with her if you went to school in Salisbury?'

'Sort of. But it wouldn't have been weekends.'

Tansy grabbed the straw she'd been handed.

'You'd have liked to stay with her weekends as well?'

'I might.'

Tansy felt like hitting her. It was often like this; there was frequently an initial reluctance to talk.

'How many bedrooms in your house, Sarah?' she asked.

'Three.'

'You have one, your parents have one, so———'

'No. We all have one each.' Sarah roughly shoved a doll into each bedroom of the house.

'What made you take that twenty pence from the boy's pocket, Sarah? Did you really need the money?'

Sarah shrugged again. 'I don't know.'

'And you took a box of paper-clips from a shop and stood outside the door until the assistant came and fetched you back. Why?'

'I don't know!' Tansy sensed tears were near to the surface. She felt she was being cruel, but she had to probe further. She picked up the father doll and examined it.

'Were you hoping to get caught, Sarah? Why? What did you think they'd do to you?'

'Send me to prison,' muttered Sarah.

'Do they send children to prison? Do you really want to leave home so badly, Sarah? Who makes you feel like this?'

Tansy put the father doll in the bedroom with the Sarah doll. Sarah stared at it without speaking, but her breathing quickened.

'Is there an uncle who lives with your aunt, Sarah?' Tansy asked gently. Sarah shook her head, as tears started to fall down her thin cheeks.

'So you'd have lived in a house alone with your aunt. And no men in the house at all?'

Sarah shuddered. She reached out and pulled the father doll from the bed and threw it across the room. Tansy knew she'd got a big task ahead. And she hadn't jumped to conclusions. She handed a tissue to Sarah.

'Come and sit by me, Sarah, and let's talk about things.'

*   *   *

The last patient had gone. Tansy checked her notes and closed the file. For a moment she sat in her chair, her elbows on the desk. And she wished an aspirin could take away the ache inside her—a deep, desperate ache of loss.

Slowly she got up and began to clear away the toys, the dolls from the dolls' house, the Lego, the wax crayons. She reached into the doll box, and her eyes widened. Sitting next to the mummy doll in dark blue, the doll who was called She, was a small green plastic frog. A Kermit frog. Tansy couldn't help feeling it was significant. Gemma had placed her most cherished toy next to a peson who wasn't even a memory, just the woman who had given her away. Could she still be hoping for a miracle? Tansy couldn't help feeling warm inside. Yet it was too late. The miracle would never happen.

She took the frog in her hand. It was slightly tacky, as though Gemma had handled it with sticky fingers. Gemma's. But she couldn't keep it, however much she longed to. She was hardly aware of the soft tear that slid gently down her cheek.

Someone knocked at the door, and she jumped up and hurried to open it. A staff nurse, in blue uniform, stood there. Tansy was sure she'd seen her around the hospital, and in the dining-room. She was small, plump, and wore large round spectacles.

'Dr Blair?' Casually Tansy glanced at her name badge, and gasped. The girl noticed it, and nodded.

'May I come in? It's Tansy, isn't it?'

Speechless, Tansy closed the door behind them. 'Christina Swallow,' she managed to say, her throat dry.

'I'm sorry it took so long,' said the girl. 'But I looked everywhere for you.'

'Why?' asked Tansy shortly.

'Because I knew you'd think all the wrong things about Rod and me.'

'Were they wrong?' retorted Tansy. 'He said he was going to Reading, alone. And he was found near Andover with you, conveniently near to the expensive private clinic your father owns. Where you recovered from your injuries, I suppose.'

She slumped in her chair. She didn't need all this pain on top of her present agony. Christina sat opposite, her round blue eyes watching her.

'No,' the girl said softly, shaking her head. 'I said you'd got it all wrong. I wanted to tell you, but I was in a coma for weeks, and it took me months to get fit again.' She smiled at Tansy's horrified expression.

'I was in Salisbury General, actually. I was too ill to be moved. Anyway I quite liked it there. I made a lot of friends, and decided to take up nursing as soon as I was well enough. And that took me two years.'

'I'm sorry to hear you were so badly injured,' said Tansy stiffly. 'But I can't see how——'

'No, I haven't explained yet,' said Christina. 'I know Rod told you he was going to Reading. It was a white lie. He couldn't tell you the truth, because he wanted to surprise you. He was on his way to a jeweller's in Andover—Alan's father. You remember Alan? Rod had asked his father to make an engagement ring for you, a special one with your favourite stones——'

'Amethysts,' whispered Tansy. Oh, yes, she was remembering it all, remembered losing a costume ring before the wedding. Had Rod taken it for her finger size? She stared at Christina's pleasant face.

'He wasn't sure about the design,' the girl went on. 'He asked my advice. He picked me up at Burbage, where I'd been staying, and we went down together. We reached Ludgershall—you know the rest. He tried to avoid a cyclist, swerved, skidded on a patch of oil, hit a tree—well, that's what they told me. I don't remember any of it.'

Tansy felt she had been turned to stone.

'He wasn't going to work for your father, at Swallow Court?' she managed to say.

Christina laughed. 'Good heavens, no! Rod was

ambitious, an idealist. He was going to be a neuro-surgeon. You must have known that.'

Tansy nodded. She was thinking of the last six years—more than six years—of remembering Rod as she had known him, yet hating him for his betrayal. He hadn't betrayed her. She had betrayed him. She hadn't trusted him, and she'd given away his last gift to her. Rosalind. Gemma.

'Thank you for coming,' she said through dry lips.

'I tried to find you before, but you weren't there,' Christina went on. 'It was about Easter, I think—April. I went home to London. Then I went to Newcastle to train. I came here last year, to be nearer my family. Dr Vernon told me you were working here, so here I am. I'm glad I've found you. Six years is a long time to carry bitterness.'

She stood up, and Tansy noticed an ugly scar running down her neck.

'You've come six years too late,' she said softly, opening her hand and looking at the small green frog.

CHAPTER THIRTEEN

As soon as she reached her flat, Tansy took the little green frog from her bag and placed it on the hall table. She could hardly wait to see Gemma's joyful expression.

She was expected at eight. With a feeling of alarm, she realised she should have brought Gemma's notes with her. This was supposed to be a professional meeting, not a social one. But it didn't matter. She could remember every detail of her meetings with Gemma, almost down to the last word.

She smiled to herself. She hoped Nicholas didn't find that unusual. She'd eaten a sandwich at the hospital before leaving, so all she had to do now was shower and change into something suitable. She chose a plain linen dress in mauve. The weather was quite warm for early May.

At half-past seven the phone rang. She put down her hairbrush and answered it.

'Tansy? Nicholas here. I'm at the hospital. The Prof called an urgent meeting on ward safety, so I may be a little late. But don't wait for me. Beth will give you a drink before she leaves. And you can always reassure yourself that Gemma's not at death's door!'

He gave a little laugh, and Tansy wondered if there was an ulterior motive for that remark. I'm getting paranoid, she thought, as she put down the phone.

She tucked the little frog into her white shoulder bag and left the flat. During the short drive to Ascot Avenue, the feeling grew stronger that this visit was in some way going to be important. And she was determined not to let Nicholas see she was upset because they were leaving Swindon.

Beth let her in. She was wearing black trousers and a cream silk shirt. She slipped on a black velvet jacket as

Tansy came in. Tansy couldn't help feeling rather drab in her mauve dress and white sandals.

'I'm glad you're early, Tansy,' smiled Beth. 'I couldn't leave until you came, because of Gemma. And Nicholas is going to be late.'

'Yes, I know—he rang me. Is Gemma asleep?'

'I shouldn't imagine so. I told her you were coming and she was quite excited. Oh, you found her frog! She'll be thrilled. Yes, you must take it up to her. Oh, and help yourself to a drink, won't you?'

'Thanks—perhaps later.' Tansy moved towards the stairs. Beth put out a hand.

'Tansy, I suppose you know she's very fond of you? Talks about you all the time. And I remembered you saying once you intended to make medicine your whole life. Well, I think you'd make an excellent mother, that's all.'

Tansy stiffened. 'That's not the issue, Beth. I've come here tonight to discuss Gemma, not my future.'

'I'm talking about Gemma,' said Beth. 'She needs a mother.'

'Then it's Nicholas you should——'

'Connie told me, Tansy. She told me everything— Rod, the baby, the adoption. Everything.'

Tansy couldn't answer. The moment she had been dreading had arrived.

'You must have known she would have, Tansy.'

Tansy nodded. 'I don't suppose it matters any longer.'

Beth moved towards her. 'Tansy, all I want to say is I think you were incredibly brave. I know I couldn't do it. But it will never happen to me. I shall never have children, because of the HC. It wouldn't be fair.'

The implications of that remark passed over Tansy's head. She could only think of Nicholas knowing all the time—surely he had known?

'What did Nicholas say about—the baby?' Her voice came out as a croak. Beth's eyes widened.

'I haven't told Nicholas. Why should I? I only told him about Rod, and that was because I could see he was serious about you.' Her voice softened. 'It must have been tragic for you, Tansy, losing someone you loved, then going through the trauma of birth, for someone else.'

'Why?' asked Tansy.

'Why what?'

'Why didn't you tell Nicholas? It would have made it easier for you.'

'Your logic defeats me, Tansy. I guessed it was something you felt very sensitive about. The way you denied your mother, for a start. So you haven't told him?'

Tansy shook her head. 'And I don't intend to. I'd rather not talk about it.' She glanced around the hall. 'This is such a lovely house, Beth. You should get a good price for it.'

Beth paused as she opened the front door. 'It's not up for sale,' she said.

'But you'll be in Scotland—— Oh, are you renting it out? I only wish I could afford it!' exclaimed Tansy.

'And I wish I knew what you were talking about,' said Beth. 'But I'm afraid I have to dash. We'll talk about it another time.'

'There won't be another time,' Tansy called out softly, but the front door had closed. She stood in the hall, holding the frog. She'd been right. It was proving to be a momentous evening, even before it had started.

With a mixture of joy and sadness, she went upstairs and quietly opened Gemma's door. The curtains were half drawn, but the room was still light. Gemma lay turned away from her, one arm above her head, her eyes closed. Sadly, because she would have liked to see the child one more time, Tansy laid the frog softly on the bedside table. Gemma's eyes flicked open, and she turned quickly.

'Dr Tansy! I've been waiting for you!'

'I'm sorry if I woke you.' It seemed so natural to bend

and kiss the sweet-smelling cheek. 'I've brought your Kermit back.'

'Kermit! But I wasn't asleep, Dr Tansy. I was just sort of dreaming. I was thinking about you.' Gemma took the frog and put him under her pillow.

'I'm very flattered,' smiled Tansy. 'Weren't you dreaming about Scotland?'

'Oh, I've been there before, lots of times.'

'I shall miss seeing you.' You'll never know how much, Tansy thought.

'Don't I have to come to the hospital any more? I thought I had to come for the loose ends and things. You told my daddy that. What does it mean?' asked Gemma.

'Oh, it just means putting everything straight. So that's why I've come tonight.' Tansy hugged her. 'But you're sleepy, and your daddy will be very cross if I keep you awake.'

'Can't you stay with me for a few minutes? I'm not tired.'

'Oh, all right.'

The child snuggled against her, sighing happily. 'I love you, Dr Tansy.'

Tansy's heart almost burst with happiness. She kissed Gemma.

'And I love you, Gemma—such a lot.'

'Shall I send you a postcard from Scotland?'

'I'd like that very much.'

'We shall be staying with Grannie,' Gemma told her. 'She lives in Kilmarnock. And I've got a grandpa in Wales, in a place with a funny name.'

Tansy smiled. She wanted to tell her about her other grannie in Carolina, but knew she never could.

'Where did you find Kermit?' asked Gemma sleepily.

'Don't you remember where you'd put him? In the doll box, next to the other mummy doll—She.'

'She wasn't a real mummy,' said Gemma, 'because she didn't want to keep me.'

'Oh, but she did, Gemma! I know she did,' said Tansy earnestly.

'Then why did she give me away?'

'Because—oh, because of lots of things.' Because she was a coward, she was afraid to be reminded of pain. But the pain stayed with her. 'Come closer, Gemma, and I'll tell you all about her. I'll try to explain it all so you'll understand properly.'

Gemma obediently tucked herself next to Tansy, and Tansy put her arm around her. Although her heart was breaking, this was a moment she knew she would remember for the rest of her life.

'Your other grandpa, in Scotland, he died a long time ago, from a nasty illness that lasted years and years. Your second mummy thought she'd got the same illness, and she didn't want to be a worry to everyone, having to look after her, especially you. So she decided to—well, end it all quickly. She knew you'd be happy with your daddy and Aunt Beth. I suppose she expected your Aunt Beth to be your new mummy.'

Her throat felt so tight, speaking was physically painful.

'But why can't you be my new mummy?'

'I'm sorry, Gemma, it's just not possible——'

'You said you loved me a lot!'

'I do, Gemma.'

'Why can't I have a mummy who loves me a lot?' It was a cry from the heart, and Tansy sought for the right words.

'Your first mummy loved you a lot, so much——'

'How do you know?' the child demanded. 'Have you spoken to her?'

'In a way.'

Gemma looked up at her with round eyes, such a deep, deep blue, like pansies, like that baby so many years ago. . . 'Where is she?'

'Not far away.'

'Tell me about her.'

'She was young, only twenty, and she was a student at university. And she fell in love with a young doctor called Rod. Rod had black curly hair——'

'Like mine!'

'Just like yours, and he laughed a lot. And he was going to marry your mummy——' Tansy's heart suddenly swelled as she realised this was all perfectly true, always had been true. . . 'But before you were born, he was killed in a car accident, and your mummy couldn't look after you on her own. She didn't want to give you up, she loved you more than anyone else in the world, but she wanted you to be happy, so she decided to give you to a mummy and daddy who couldn't have their own children, and it made them very happy.'

There was silence in the room. Downstairs a clock chimed the half hour. The landing outside creaked as the house settled for the night.

'Did she cry, Dr Tansy?' asked Gemma in a small voice.

'She broke her heart, Gemma. She wanted to keep her Rosalind for herself. She's never forgotten you. She thinks about you all the time.'

'You called me Rosalind the other day,' Gemma remembered.

'That's right. Your name was Rosalind.'

'Does she look like me?'

'Only her eyes. Your daddy had black hair. She has sort of yellow hair, like corn——'

'Like yours, Dr Tansy!'

'Yes, like mine.'

'What did she do after she gave me away? Did she marry someone else?'

'No, Gemma. She was very upset after Rod died. She became a doctor, and now she works with children who are unhappy.'

'You work with children who are unhappy, Dr Tansy. You told me once.' Gemma frowned. 'Was I unhappy?'

'I think you must have been, because you heard things you didn't understand. I think we've got them straight now, don't you?' said Tansy.

'Mm-hm. I wish you could be my mummy——'

'No, Gemma, it's not possible. It would mean—well, telling people things that would only hurt them.'

'But you love me. And you love my daddy——'

'When did I say that?' asked Tansy, astonished.

'You kissed him. I saw you, you had your arms round his neck, like I do when I kiss him. It was that other time you came here. I went downstairs for a glass of milk, and I saw you.'

'Gemma, a kiss doesn't mean——'

'But you do love him, don't you? I know he loves you, I heard him saying——'

'Please, Gemma, no more!' begged Tansy. 'Yes, you're right, of course I love him, more than he'll ever know. But you're all going to Scotland, and I shall be down here. I don't suppose I shall see—any of you—again.'

Her voice broke on the last words. Gemma stared at her in amazement.

'You're crying, Dr Tansy! Is it because you love my daddy? Please don't cry!'

'No, I'm not really crying——' sniffed Gemma.

'Well, I agree with Gemma. I think you are.'

'Nicholas! How long have you been standing there?' Tansy jumped up from the bed, her face flushed. How much had he overheard?

'Just a few minutes. Long enough.'

'Then I can't see any point in staying any longer.' Her worst fears had been realised. Trying to control her turbulent, confused emotions, Tansy refused to look at him, turning to Gemma instead and holding the child's hand with more ferocity than she was aware of.

'I just came up to return Gemma's frog, and say goodbye to her——' She realised she was squeezing the child's hand, and released it.' And I stayed to tell her—a fairy story.'

'Goodbye? A fairy story?' echoed Nicholas. 'Look at me, Tansy. What are you talking about?'

'Do I have to spell it out?' A quick glance revealed not the anger she expected to see on his face, but a worried, puzzled expression.

'In words of one syllable, I should imagine. You're not making sense. But there's something I have to do first. Not here. Come on, Gemma, time you were fast asleep. Say goodnight to Dr Tansy.'

Tansy bent and kissed her. She was reluctant to release the child's clasp on her neck.

'Wasn't it the truth, Dr Tansy? About She? Was it just a story?' Gemma whispered loudly. It was obvious Nicholas would hear the reply. Well, it didn't matter now. Nothing mattered.

'The whole truth, darling,' she said quietly, and the words seemed to echo in the quiet room. Or was it just in her head? 'Sleep tight. God bless.'

She tucked in the child's arm and followed Nicholas out of the room, dreading the confrontation that was bound to come.

Nicholas waited on the landing. As soon as the door was closed behind her, he pulled her into his arms, his lips seeking hers, and her initial resistance soon melted under the heat of his kisses, the warmth of his hands through her thin clothes, and the tingling, like an electric current, that ran through her from head to toe. A little bit of her was still trying to reason logically, but her brain didn't seem to be functioning, and the words she knew she should be saying, the protests, wouldn't reach her lips. Not that it mattered now. He knew everything—so why was he kissing her like this, as if he meant it, as if he never wanted to let her go? She struggled free.

'Nicholas—please—this isn't right——'

'Ssh! Wait. Don't say a word.' Holding her hand, he led her across the landing to his own room, that yellow, sunny room. He sat her on the edge of the bed, and drew up a chair.

'Tell me,' he said, taking her hand.

Tansy was still looking for the horror and shame that her story must have aroused in him. But he just looked concerned. And sad.

'But you've heard it all,' she faltered. 'And you weren't supposed to know.'

'About Gemma? Or about loving me?'

She flushed. 'If I hadn't come tonight, you'd have gone to Scotland, and that would have been the end of it. Can't we pretend I never came?'

'Tansy, it's too late for pretending. You—what did you mean by 'the end of it'? Did you think I wasn't coming back?'

'Beth said you were staying there.'

'Beth is staying there. Gemma and I are coming back by train on Tuesday. I have a job to go to, don't forget. And I was trying to pluck up enough courage to ask you to come with us.'

'You can't mean that—not now you know about me. You should hate me.'

'How could I ever hate you? I just don't understand why you didn't tell me all this before. You told me about Rod, but I sensed there was more. Didn't you trust me?'

'I was afraid,' she whispered, and Nicholas came and sat beside her, drawing her against him. She rested her head on his shoulder. 'I trusted once, and I believed I'd been let down, betrayed. Christina came and told me what had really happened, and I realised then I'd spent six years in bitter disillusionment, six years when I could have been living.'

'It's not too late to change,' he said softly, nuzzling her neck.

'I jumped to conclusions,' she agreed. 'But what was I to think? I'd seen Gemma's birthmark, and that made it harder. Not only did I have to give you up, but I had to give her up yet again.'

'Rosalind. That was when I knew. She came home on Tuesday and said you'd called her Rosalind. "Hello again, Rosalind," you'd said. She thought it was funny, but I knew what it meant.'

'Oh, of course—her birth certificate!'

'Only June and I knew she'd been registered as Rosalind,' Nicholas told her. 'I wanted to keep the name. But June wanted Gemma, and Rosemary after an old friend, so I went along with it.'

Thinking of June reminded Tansy of Beth. She looked up at him.

'You know Beth still loves you?'

He sighed. 'I suppose she does. I suppose that's why she's going away again. As she did before.'

'I don't think I could be as brave,' murmured Tansy.

'When you did the bravest thing any woman could do, give away her child?'

'It was because of cowardice,' said Tansy quickly. 'And shame. I was ashamed of my murky past. I wasn't even brave enough to tell you to your face.' She looked up at him again. 'I loved you from the start, Nicholas. I tried to deny it; I was afraid I'd lose you if I told you. And I knew I couldn't marry you if I didn't.'

'But my love was strong enough for both of us, Tansy.' He kissed her fingertips. 'And how can you call Gemma a "murky past"? She was our miracle. June adored her. Tansy, you had no reason to feel ashamed.'

'I can't help feeling Beth's surrender was more unselfish than mine.' His feather-light kisses were sending tingles up her arms.

'Surrender is such an emotive word,' he said, kissing her neck where a pulse beat rapidly. 'What does it mean to you, Tansy?'

She had hardly been aware that he had gently unbuttoned her dress and was now sliding it over her hips. She felt she could hardly breathe as his hands moved over her body, stroking her breasts and her neck. The fire which had smouldered inside her, the fire she had tried so hard to put out, seemed to flare up and engulf her, until she couldn't hear for the roaring in her ears, couldn't feel anything but the glorious ecstasy in her veins, and the fulfilment that surrender brought.

'I came to talk about Gemma,' she murmured, between his kisses.

'We've got a lifetime for that,' Nicholas replied. 'A lifetime.'

While away the lazy days of late Summer with our new gift selection
Intimate Moments

Four Romances, new in paperback, from four favourite authors.
The perfect treat!

The Colour of the Sea
Rosemary Hammond

The Heron Quest
Charlotte Lamb

Had We Never Loved
Jeneth Murrey

Magic of the Baobab
Yvonne Whittal

Available from July 1991. Price: £6.40

4 MEDICAL ROMANCES
AND 2 FREE GIFTS
From Mills & Boon

Capture all the excitement, intrigue and emotion of the busy medical world by accepting four FREE Medical Romances, plus a FREE cuddly teddy and special mystery gift. Then if you choose, go on to enjoy 4 more exciting Medical Romances every month! Send the coupon below at once to:

**MILLS & BOON READER SERVICE, FREEPOST
PO BOX 236, CROYDON, SURREY CR9 9EL.**
No stamp required

✂ - - - - - - - - - - - - - - - - - ✂

YES! Please rush me my 4 Free Medical Romances and 2 Free Gifts! Please also reserve me a Reader Service Subscription. If I decide to subscribe, I can look forward to receiving 4 Medical Romances every month for just £5.80 delivered direct to my door. Post and packing is free, and there's a free Mills & Boon Newsletter. If I choose not to subscribe I shall write to you within 10 days – I can keep the books and gifts whatever I decide. I can cancel or suspend my subscription at any time. I am over 18.

EP02D

Name (Mr/Mrs/Ms) _____

Address _____

_____

_____ Postcode _____

Signature _____